GERMAN

JUSTICE

GERMAN

JUSTICE

MARCUS

FEDDER

First published in 2020
by Black Spring Press
Suite 333, 19-21 Crawford Street
Marylebone, London W1H 1PJ
United Kingdom

Cover design by Daniel Benneworth-Gray
Typeset by Edwin Smet

All rights reserved
Copyright © 2020 by Marcus Fedder

The right of Marcus Fedder to be identified as author of
this work has been asserted in accordance with section 77
of the Copyright, Designs and Patents Act 1988

ISBN 978-1-913606-27-5

This book is a work of fiction. The characters, incidents, and dialogue
are drawn from the author's imagination and are not to be construed
as real. Any resemblance to actual events or persons, living or dead,
is entirely coincidental.

(…)
I realised that the Nuremberg trials had only dealt with a few cases. The vast majority of Nazis lived on, many SS murderers, as if nothing had happened. Many of the Nazi machine had been integrated into the new German bureaucracy. How many judges got disqualified?
– Max Hardenberg

Born in 1959, Fedder grew up in Germany where discussions of WW2 were part of his childhood. He lived for many years in London, working as a banker in development finance. In 2008, Fedder published his first novel *Sarabande*, set in Sarajevo during the war of 1992. *German Justice* is his second novel. Marcus Fedder studied International Relations at FU Berlin, LSE and Cambridge, lives in the Swiss mountains and with the proceeds of his art supports the UK Charity Children of the Mekong.

Mazurka.

F. CHOPIN. Op. 63, No 3.

Preface 2010

'Of all the stuff Mum is playing, this Mazurka is still her best. She's playing it tonight, isn't she?' Mischa takes her earphones out of her ears and puts them into mine. 'Here, listen to it. It's the Deutsche Gramophone recording.' I close my eyes as I listen to the music and memories sweep back. My daughter knows the effect this music has on me.

'It's about time you published your story, Dad,' Mischa says with a warm smile as I take the earphones out and the train pulls into Mainz station. She pauses briefly, looking out of the window, as if thinking. 'Wasn't it here in Mainz that you shot that SS creep?' I nod. 'You're smiling, Dad, this innocent and ironic smile.'

She leans back in her seat, her long dark hair falling over her shoulders. With her eyes closed my daughter hardly passes as a twenty-year-old. She's sitting relaxed, her feet up on the seat opposite her. 'Tell me again, how you did it,' she insists.

It all seemed to have gone so fast that even today I cannot believe what actually happened. Twenty years have passed but I still remember that scene as if it happened yesterday.

'I've told you many times, Mischa, but now I can't, it was too awful.'

'You mean how his whole body suddenly froze just before you pulled the trigger and how he collapsed, like in a slow-motion movie? Hmm. I guess you are right, Dad, you are awful.'

We both look out of the window for a while. The passing platform is empty except for one woman, staring intently through the window into the waiting room.

'But sometimes you can only get real justice when a chapter is properly closed,' I add.

'No remorse then, I sense,' Mischa says.

'No, definitely no remorse.'

'You're horrible, Dad,' she adds, sitting up in her chair. 'But I'm glad you are finally telling your story. You have to add this chapter to the script, Dad. It's so convincing.'

'Not sure, sweetheart. I don't want to tell the whole world about it.'

'But nobody will believe you anyway, Dad. Promise me to tell the whole story,' Mischa insists after a while.

'Why?'

'So that everyone knows how difficult the issue of justice is.'

I sit in silence and look at my daughter whose face has turned serious.

'Promise, Dad?' she asks.

'I promise.'

1943

I was not particularly worried about partisans attacking us. Nonetheless, I was trying to drive fast. I glanced to my right where Mischa was sitting. He seemed to be sleeping despite the fact that he got shaken around as we were swerving between the tracks that were left by our tanks. Most days we were thirsty. I looked around as we approached the forest on the right, which, despite the heat was lush and dark green. On the left were acres of endless fields. Mischa opened one eye.

'Ukraine is definitely tank country,' he observed.

We felt the wind in our faces, as our Kübelwagen was open. Mischa leant forward, trying to see what lay ahead. He grabbed my arm: 'Max, slow down,' he shouted, as I took in what he had seen.

'No, I'm not going to stop,' I hissed.

'Are you blind? It's those SS shits. I don't want to have anything to do with them.'

'Me neither, Max. I just want to stop to check what's happening.'

'You're insane...' I hesitated but slowed down. Mischa was not only my closest friend but also my commanding officer, so I had to obey.

'Stop right here, before they can hear us,' Mischa ordered. I stopped the Jeep in the shade at the edge of the forest and climbed out.

'God, Mischa, you're always looking for trouble.' I was annoyed.

We moved carefully up the hundred yards to the house, staying in the shadow of the trees. I heard the twigs cracking underneath my boots. The grey front door was open and I could hear a woman's screaming coming from inside the house.

Instantly, I ducked and rushed forward towards the back of the house. Mischa was just behind me. Reaching the low window we peeked inside. What we saw paralysed both of us. A pool of blood covered the ground. Two women were lying on the floor, an older one on her stomach, and a younger one on her back. Both looked dead.

Two SS officers were on the bed, one pinning down a young girl, the other struggling to rape her. The girl was struggling too, fighting back, crying in fear. I recognised him. The man who was pinning the girl down was Müller.

'Let's go. We can't do anything.' Mischa turned away. I was paralysed, watching the scene like in a movie. Suddenly Müller looked up and saw me. He seemed unsure of what to do.

My paralysis stopped instantaneously. I pulled my gun and fired, hitting the SS officer who was raping the girl. Two shots into his back finished him off. My third shot was aimed at Müller, but he too had pulled his gun. We both shot at the same time. His bullet strafed the wooden window frame and hit my left shoulder. I was struck by immense pain and just managed to fire another shot before dropping the gun. I could see how he slumped down and fell off the bed. Then I felt Mischa's hand as he pulled me away from the window.

'Max, what the hell are you doing?' Mischa shouted.

'I killed those bastards.'

'You idiot. You'll be court-martialled.'

'No, I killed them,' I just managed to say between clenched teeth. 'You're the only witness.'

Mischa let go of me and ran into the house. I knelt down in pain. When he came out again, he looked even paler.

'Moser and Müller. This is trouble,' he said. 'You killed Moser, but Müller is still alive. I can't believe you killed Moser. Damn it, Max.'

'I'm glad I did. But wait...' I stopped to breathe. The pain from my shoulder was terrible. Thoughts were racing around my head.

'Müller is still alive, you said?'

Mischa looked at me and nodded. 'Unconscious.'

Instantly I realised what I had to do. 'I'm going to kill him too,' I hissed, trying to get up.

Mischa grabbed my shoulder. A burning pain shot down my side. I collapsed. 'Mischa, don't.'

I tried to get up again but couldn't. 'I've got to kill the swine.'

'No. No way.'

'Mischa, what about the girl?'

'She'll be OK.'

'If Müller wakes up, she's dead. You have to kill Müller.'

'No, Max, I can't,' he said.

I felt blood pulsing in my head and blood running down my shirt. 'Then don't stop me killing him,' I whispered, sitting up, but the sky turned black all around me and I felt myself fading. I could hear Mischa but I could not see anything.

'I'll get the Jeep,' Mischa said. I could feel the pain and, as I was lying on the floor, gradually the blackness lifted and I could see again. I started crawling through the grass towards the front door, determined to finish off Müller but Mischa was faster, approaching in the Jeep. He got out, leaving the engine running, grabbed me and heaved me onto the seat. I had no strength left to struggle. As we were accelerating past the house, the girl came running out, dishevelled and disoriented.

'Oh God, poor thing,' Mischa said, looking back. I looked down at my legs and realised I was shaking violently. 'I should have shot Müller first. I'm such an idiot.'

I felt sick and angry with myself and vomited all over my legs, passing out when we hit an enormous pothole.

I woke up on a stretcher in a field hospital. The first thing I noticed, even before I could see anything, was that my arm was hurting like hell. I wasn't sure whether I could move but did not feel like trying. Then, gradually, my vision returned and I looked down my side and saw that my bandages were soaked in blood. Flies were everywhere, on the blood, on my arms, on my face, on my dirty bare feet that I could see sticking out at the other end. I was relieved to see I could still move my toes. I closed my eyes again and then, gradually, I started taking in the noise. Moaning, whimpering, crying. And then, suddenly, I noticed the smells: unbearable stench. It hit me like a wave. I tried to look around, but lifting my head shot streaks of pain into my shoulder. Above me was the canvas of a tent, a huge tent, I thought, and let my head roll back. I couldn't care less and remained in a state of half dozing for at least another two hours, trying to shut off my senses. I looked around defying the pain. The tent was full of men on stretchers. Most men were lying motionless, dazed in stupor. Everyone was covered in bandages, in dirt and dried blood. Both my neighbours were either sleeping or unconscious. Or dead. When a nurse passed by, she gave me some water to drink. It tasted beautifully clear and fresh, like mountain water, I thought. She smiled and I realised this meant more to me than the water. I had to close my eyes again and cried.

I don't remember distinctly what happened next, only that I drifted in and out of the world, sometimes it was bright, sometimes it was dark, but I was not sure whether it was because it was night or because my consciousness was impaired. Then, it was clearly day and I realised that I was just dazing in pain, thinking of nothing. Lying there, I tried to remember what had happened but had difficulty putting the pieces of the puzzle together: the shooting, getting hit, the girl, yes, the girl.

Then one day, Mischa turned up unexpectedly. I was awake, feeling better, having been able to eat some soup and drink a lot of water.

'What the heck are you doing here?'

I was still unable to sit up. Lifting my head was painful.

'Day off. Recently did a spot of overtime, so got a day off and decided to visit you. But, damn it, Max, this place stinks.'

'Ha-ha.'

I paused and looked at his face. His blue eyes were as usual full of mischief.

'Tell me, Mischa. Is Müller dead?'

'Well,' he looked around to see whether anyone could her us, 'I went into the house and checked them out. Moser was dead. But Müller was still breathing. Don't know where you got him, but he wasn't even bleeding badly.'

'Mischa, you should have shot him.'

'I just couldn't kill him, Max. Sorry.'

'What about the women?'

'Both were dead. Butchered. I tried to comfort the girl. She was,' he paused, searching for words. 'What can I say? She just remained sitting there on the edge of the bed, crying silently.'

Again he paused, looking at me for a long time. I felt bile enter my mouth and let the bitter saliva flow down my cheek. Mischa looked away. 'But you may be lucky,' he continued. 'Müller can't have recognised you, as the sun was right behind you. You could have been any partisan.'

'Do you know what happened to him?' Mischa looked at me and grabbed a dirty towel from another chair and wiped my face. It stank.

'No idea. He's probably lying in the row next to you.'

'Don't joke.'

'No, seriously,' Mischa said, 'I checked. He isn't here. No idea what happened to him. I just hope the girl is OK.'

'You should have killed him, Mischa,' I said again. I had to say it. I felt it.

Again, he looked at me as I was clutching my wounded shoulder, and then away, over the rows of stretchers. He looked pensive and I knew what he was going to say even before he opened his mouth.

'I just couldn't shoot him in cold blood,' Mischa whispered, shaking his head and looking deflated. 'I know I should have simply pulled the trigger, but I couldn't. I'm sorry.'

I felt awkward. Mischa was such a decent human being. Definitely in contrast to me.

'No need to be sorry, Mischa,' I said.

'I needed to take care of you though. I realised you'd be dead if I didn't get you to a medic soon.'

'And how did you explain that I had a German bullet in my shoulder?'

'Werner took care of you. He didn't ask any questions, but I think he figured out himself that it would be better not to ask anything. Once he'd got the bullet out, he sent you here.'

I felt tears come to my eyes, I didn't know why, and turned my head, wiping them away.

'Thanks, Mischa. You saved my life. It's OK you didn't shoot that SS creep. He deserved it, but you're too goddamn decent to kill.' I stopped and looked at him. His face was dark, his eyes shrunk back into their sockets, his lips were thin. But then he looked at me and sighed.

'Thou shalt not kill,' he said.

Again, I was overcome by emotions and now my tears just flowed freely. In the end I said: 'Yes, Mischa. Commandments are fine when the world is normal. But I wanted justice. Now.'

I paused to reflect and then continued, 'and killing those two was my understanding of justice.' Mischa pulled out a small hipflask and we each took a long sip of wonderful warm and biting vodka.

'An eye for an eye. A tooth for a tooth, I would have blown his brains out.'

1990

I have always been one hundred per cent sure that during that evening in the field hospital I wrote a letter to my mother. In it I explained to her what had happened, and why I killed, why I had to kill. That I wrote to her about the need for justice in our lives, about the need to defend the weak, the helpless. But now, sitting here in front of the fireplace, thinking back, I was not sure anymore whether I had really written it or, if I had, whether I had actually sent it and whether my mother had ever received it. I know I was delirious from vodka and from pain. It would have been immensely naïve to send such a letter as letters got censored. Had anyone read that letter, I would have been court-martialled.

I put two more logs onto the fire and watched them burn. Outside, light rain was falling on to the street. I could hear my neighbour parking his Porsche. My pipe felt cold and I took a burning twig to relight it. The smell of tobacco gradually filled the room. Years ago I smoked cigars but gave up after some time as I could not bear the stench in my living room the following morning. Cigars have a wonderful taste but smell horribly for most of the rest of the world. The thoughts of my shooting Müller had brought back more memories. For years I had forced myself to forget, had blocked the war, the killing, the horrors out of my mind, concentrating on the present. But now the memories caught up with me again as I had time to sit and think and look at the burning logs. I recently retired and all of a sudden, when you retire, you have hours, days, when you can sit and procrastinate, think and watch logs burning in the fire place.

I retired when I turned 65. On my birthday, on the 10th of April. In 1990, to be precise. I had absolutely no idea of what to do next. I did not want to retire. I loved what I was doing: Judging. Sending criminals to jail, acquitting the innocent. I saw no reason to retire. I was still young, mentally and physically top fit. When I looked into the mirror, a pair of blue-grey piercing eyes stared back. Yes, my hair was greyish-grey, and very short, but I never had long hair. I could still ski faster than most twenty-somethings and, above all, I was a good judge. "Fair, experienced, tough", the Court had said in their retirement eulogy. I did not need praise. No appeals court had ever overturned any of my judgements. I thus considered it heretically unfair to get bundled off into retirement.

I had no family to spend time with.

Being retired was thus like a judgement. Guilty. But of what? Age? My mind wandered off again and I put another log onto the fire.

I had become a judge late in my life, when I turned forty, and had been on the bench for twenty-five years. For twenty-five years I got up in the morning, shaved, had breakfast, a croissant, a double espresso, a banana, and left my apartment at twenty minutes to eight and walked to work.

On my first day of retirement, I decided it was like a Saturday. I got up, shaved, had my croissant and double espresso, bought the morning papers and sat down to read a book about international law. The second day was the same routine as on the first. Now I pretended it was Sunday.

That evening I got bitter and annoyed. When I was annoyed, I became destructive. So I ventured up to the attic and decided to clear it out. In a corner I found boxes of long-forgotten books and decided to take them downstairs and started reading till late at night.

On the third day I came across piles of useless papers, and a big brown envelope marked 'Max's Letters.' It was my mother's handwriting. I locked up the attic, went downstairs, started a fire in the fireplace and re-lit my pipe. I watched as the smoke went up in bluish rings, and, crouching down in front of the fireplace, opened the envelope.

I found my letters, those letters I had sent my mother from the front, from Russia and Ukraine. My mother had folded them neatly and put them into one bundle. I had no idea how they got there, maybe Lisa, my sister, had saved them when our house burnt down. I did not send any letters during the years I spent as a prisoner of war in Russian camps.

My mother had died in the bombings.

I read what I had written and memories flashed up again. I saw myself in the APC, the armoured personnel carrier. I remembered again the constant fear and, closing my eyes, I felt it creeping back into my body. I heard the sounds, the thuds of our artillery, the crushing noise, when the Soviet shells hit the ground nearby, the staccato of machine gun fire. I will always remember the shelling, the shooting, the killing.

Most of my friends did not survive, but I was lucky. So was my friend Mischa. When our first APC got hit and destroyed, I was outside, searching for water, whilst my friends burnt to death. A shell killed Olaf, who was my best friend then. I sat back and closed my eyes again, but no, I first had to get up and fill up my glass of whisky. Lagavulin. I needed the taste of peat and smoke.

I sat back and thought. How unfair things were that they did not let us finish school. We were just eighteen when we got drafted in 1943 and the war seemed practically lost but not yet over. Thinking about it now, I realise that, in a way I was lucky that I could stay at school for such a long time. Others had been drafted much younger. But the fact that my dad had died at the beginning of the war, probably helped. I had been secretly hoping that I might not have to fight at all anymore, that the Allies would over-run the last defences and destroy Hitler's Armies in the East and in the West.

But we got drafted. And once we were drafted, we were designated cannon fodder. Our training was minimal and, already in late spring, things got real. Being a natural coward, I had been hoping till the end to be sent to occupy Greece, Holland or France, but my hopes were dashed as cannon fodder was needed in the East.

I was a simple soldier in the Army, as were most of my friends. Mischa was an exception in so far as he was both an officer and then also became a friend, my best friend, in fact, after Olaf had died. Our friendship continued once the war was over. Although none of us supported the Nazi ideology, we were fighting. There was no doubt about that. We were fighting to save ourselves. We were shooting at those who shot at us. I shot at soldiers storming out of their trenches attacking ours. We stuck together and each time one of us died, hit by shrapnel or bullets, it was as if a part of ourselves was dying with him. It was as if our emotions, our souls, were turning into huge swathes of scar tissue, shrinking with each friend we lost. I put another log on to the fire and watched it burn as if it was burning through my past. I remembered when Olaf died.

Olaf

We had started our training together and ended up in the same company, the same platoon. It was only our second night at the front. It was pitch black and eerily quiet and yet I felt that something was not right. I raised my head just slightly out of the trench to look across to the other side where kids of our ages were sitting in their trenches. We waited in silence. The total silence is sometimes harder to bear than the noise of machine gun fire. Olaf was crouching down, about ten metres away from me, I could sense his presence in the darkness. Suddenly there was a bright flash and a shell exploded, sending shrapnel flying all over. I heard a shout and then whimpering that slowly died. I rushed over to Olaf who was lying on his back. Lighting a match I saw his face and the gaping hole that had been his left eye. His face was white with bright red blood running down the side. I held his head in my arms as he was trying to speak, but his lips moved without any noise. I don't know whether he felt any pain or whether he was already beyond pain, as he looked at me with his one blue eye which was slowly fading. Even when he was dead, he seemed to smile, whilst I was crying. I wasn't sure whether I wanted to live or to die with him and I was still crying at dawn when our sergeant pulled my arm to get me going and we moved on. Why? I stumbled forward, realising I needed to stay alive in order to help my comrades.

We stuck together. We had sworn to stick together.

Lagavulin

I loved this whisky. It tasted so much like I felt during the nights when the fighting stopped and bitterness descended upon us. I took another sip and my thoughts drifted back to my friends who fought with me, who died next to me, who were my life those days. But then I also remembered those others.

The Waffen SS. They were Germans, like me, Mischa and Olaf. But they could have been from a different planet. They walked differently, they talked differently. They killed differently. They were brutal for the sake of brutality.

They took out not only the enemy but cleaned up behind us, rounding up Jews, partisans, communists, gypsies, homosexuals, killing them on the spot or transporting them off. Where to? I often wondered – and we tried to guess. Now we all know.

My friends and I tried to stay away from them as best as we could. There were the three young SS officers, Müller, Moser and a third guy, whose paths we nonetheless crossed a number of times. Moser, I had killed.

I took another sip of Lagavulin and felt the sense of deep satisfaction arising from within. It once again brought back the scene of me shooting them through the window. Moser collapsed. My bullets had killed him instantaneously. I sometimes wondered why I felt no remorse, not then, nor today, but there could not have been remorse. I had wanted Moser and Müller to die. When I saw the bodies of the two women lying on the floor in a pool of blood, when I heard the frightened screams of the girl who was being raped, I knew I had to kill. Even many years later, when I was arguing against the death penalty at a legal symposium in The Hague, I felt that I could argue against it because I had killed in order to mete out justice. I know this is a contradiction but in war, justice is different. It is immediate, it is deadly and it is justified.

Müller, I had shot, but not killed. I remembered him as if it had happened yesterday, not only the day I shot him, but the times I had encountered him before. He was at least three to four years older than me. Blonde hair, a non-existent beard and hollow cheeks. Had you met him in the street, you would not have thought that he belonged to as brutal, vulgar and deadly an organisation as the SS. His mother probably didn't even know. Moser, in contrast, was short and chubby. Some of the SS, except for Müller, I figured, must have had complete charisma by-passes in civilian life.

When you are saddled with such visible disadvantages, you have to compensate. The trio did this by building their reputation of senseless brutality. I must admit that the Waffen SS had some officers whose reckless guts I respected. Those few were fighters and not afraid of anything. They stuck together and often managed to break through a line and destroy the other side where we had given up. But those were the minority and Moser and Müller or their third partner were certainly not part of them. This trio's specialty became cleaning up behind the lines. Cowardice. And I hated their swagger and tried to stay away from them.

Judging

In the morning I woke up wanting to go to work, only to realise that there was no work waiting for me. There are thousands of defendants waiting in limbo and the courts are too busy but they sent me into retirement. I understand that you send a pilot to the golf course when his eyesight gets too weak to fly, but my brain wasn't too weak to judge and nobody seemed to realise that I don't do golf. The espresso seemed more bitter too. I sat down, looking out of the window, where spring was starting to show with early flowers blossoming in the garden. Daffodils. I wished I could have retired in autumn, which would have felt more appropriate, when snow starts falling, covering the past. It rarely snows in April.

Cases drifted into my mind, from many years ago. I remembered the first rape trial. I was nervous. The defendant was very gentle in court, with a local accent, wearing sandals, more a hippie than a tough criminal. Not your typical rapist, if there is such a thing as a typical rapist. He had broken into the apartment of an elderly woman and then was sick enough to force her to cook him lunch, and after lunch he raped her. He claimed she had consented. Is this a normal person? But then again, no rapist is normal. He should have been sent to a loony bin. I probed into the deeper psychological reasons of his acts, his relationship with his mother and his older sister. Bullying, alcohol, drugs, abuse as a child. I felt sorry for the guy in a way, but knew nothing could justify rape. I know no leniency in such cases, just justice. I jailed him.

The second time I spent even more time examining the real reasons that led the defendant to commit such a hideous crime. The defence was marvellously eloquent. It almost sounded as if the defendant had done it for therapy. But why should someone get less years for a rape just because he loved his mother and his love was not properly returned? Maybe it would be justice to have jailed the mother too, for mucking up her son. But I jailed just him.

In both cases, I realised afterwards with some satisfaction, that it was probably for long enough that they would not be a threat to their elderly victims anymore. I don't think a victim is very interested in finding out that the aggressor acted in a certain way because of his or her childhood or upbringing. If you have been the victim of a crime, you just want justice. Which means locking up. And that was what I did. It sounds harsh, but that is what a judge is there for. It is fairness on which society is based. Only after such fairness is there space for forgiving.

I often erred on the side of leniency. *In dubio pro reo*, this short sentence determined my judging. Roman law, based upon Aristotle. I had studied Greek philosophy of law, Aristotle, Roman writings. In doubt, in favour of the accused. An incredibly short and powerful sentence.

But this law, which should form the basis of humanity, is void in war.

If in doubt, shoot. I had shot Moser and Müller. The fraction of a second I had doubted meant that Müller was able to shoot at me. In court you have time to think. In dubio pro reo.

If there is one thing I've always hated, it's unresolved cases. Criminals living free. Crime without punishment. In my whole career I only had five such cases that I could not resolve, where I had to let the defendant go free without having found the real culprit. Where crime remained unpunished. One such case was a murderer. Memories flashed back. Yes, murderer, not murder. A fifteen year old girl was murdered on her way home from school. She was about to be raped but fought back and in the fight got stabbed. There was a witness. There was the weapon. But the defendant had an alibi. He was caught by the police at a different place at about the same time, speeding. But there was a tiny speck of blood on his car. But was it his car? The witnesses then started to get muddled up when stressed by the defence. The factor time became a determining force, but for the defence. *In dubio pro reo*. I couldn't jail him. Ten months later another girl got attacked by the same man. Unfortunately for him, she was a Judo black belt and took his knife and rammed it into his chest. He died. I thought it was better justice than the jail sentence I would have given him.

I acquitted many. My definition of self-defence enraged many of my colleagues.

I saw no problem in a shopkeeper defending himself,

when he was getting burgled. If you are faced with an attacker with a knife, how much patience do you have to show? Do you really have to wait till the knife is rammed into your stomach before you knock the attacker out with a bottle of wine over his head? Do you have to wait till a dog mauls your child before you strangle the dog? The dog had bitten the child and then got killed by the kid's father. The owner was outraged and wanted to see the father jailed – I made sure the tables got turned and the owner became the defendant.

And all of this was over now. I would never again be able to set people free or send them to jail. Well, I had done it for 25 years.

The one thing I regretted was never to be able to judge a war criminal. A Nazi. I wish I had been an American judge at Nuremberg. Would I have been able to stick to the defining principle of In dubio pro reo or would I have been driven by my instinct and wartime experience and judged In dubio contra reo. I do not know. It would have been deeply satisfying though.

Mischa

In my second week of retirement, Mischa came to visit me in Munich and, immediately, I knew that he was up to something interesting. He was always beaming when he had some grandiose plans.

'Look Max,' he said, 'you know what we should do?' He looked at me, waiting for excitement, which I couldn't feel. 'What do you think of the following idea: we'll fly to Russia and trace our steps all the way back to where we were dug in, to where you joined the front the first time and maybe also go to Stalingrad.'

'Volgograd, you mean? The place I came too late to visit in '43?'

'The way we went in 1943 and 44. But this time we'll go by car rather than by foot.'

'Hmm,' I had to think back. 'What you meant is that I hiked in those days whilst you were being driven around in your bloody Kübelwagen.'

'Rubbish, Max. You know it was blown to pieces and I had to walk like everybody else.'

I remained silent. I wasn't sure whether that was my idea of retirement.

'Let me think about it,' I added. 'Maybe I prefer just to play boccia in Bologna.'

We went out to Sergio's, my local Italian restaurant, for

dinner. Sergio, the chef and owner came out to greet us.

'Usual place, Dottore?'

'Anywhere is fine,' I said.

We sat down at a table near the window and watched the people walk by. It was April but already warm outside. Inside Sergio's it was always warm – the pizza oven, the open plan kitchen, the red and blue murals, one abstract, the other with Lake Garda and some naked nymphs, which Sergio explained were all his former girlfriends. Each table was lit by candles and he always had jazz music playing in the background. Normally Stan Getz and Gilberto. I loved his cooking.

'Come to think of it,' Mischa continued once he had finished eating, 'it might be easier if we drove all the way. I don't think we'll find that many Hertz rental stations in Russia.'

'In your Jeep?'

'Sure, why not. At least I know the car and can repair it if it breaks down; and we could load everything we need into the back.'

I finished my glass of wine. Wonderfully mature Bordeaux, Chateau Leoville Barton.

'If we go and get the visa now, we could be off in two- or three-weeks' time,' Mischa said, looking at me. He knew instinctively what I was thinking, that I was hesitant.

'I'm not convinced yet.' I somewhat sulked, being confronted with Mischa's overwhelming energy. But then again, I thought it might be curious to see all those places again. And those places I never saw, like Volgograd or Kiev.

Memories that I had pushed aside for all those years came back. Not the memories of war, but of the years as a prisoner of war afterwards. War was bad but being a prisoner of war in Russia seemed to have been worse. I read all the books by Solzhenitzyn when they came out and found that the conditions in our gulag had not been much better. We did not know what we hated more, winter or summer. But in the winters, we were yearning for the summer warmth as it was ice cold. Day and night. We were freezing even when we were slaving away and freezing at night under our thin blankets. Many died in the winters and if you fell ill, you had it. But the summers brought torture from mosquitos, heat and thirst. And so we were yearning again for some cold. Stalin had scant regard for the Geneva Convention. Sometimes I even thought, maybe he was right: the fact was that Germany had been the aggressor, and a brutal and inhumane one on top of that. Every prison guard let us feel that fact. Every day. The other fact remained that Stalin himself killed probably more people in Russia than the whole of the German army managed to kill on its way into Russia and back. But I only found that out once I had returned home.

'We don't need to go as far as your prison camp, Max,' Mischa said, sensing what was going on in my mind.

I did not reply, as the thoughts continued in my mind at their own pace. Again, I could feel the pain of my empty stomach, but also the pain where I had got hit in my shoulder, my broken collar bone. I wasn't sure whether

I really wanted to return. But then again, I was thinking that it might be positive, if I could see things again, those places I had sworn myself never to return to.

I looked over to the kitchen where Sergio was working in the glow of the fire, trying to postpone the decision I had made. It did not work.

'Let's go as soon as we get the visa,' I finally said.
'Done.'

Back in the USSR

'Forget your tent, Mischa,' I said when I saw the big bag. 'I'm staying in hotels, I hate camping.'

'What, hotels in the middle of Ukraine?'

Mischa was probably right, I had to concede. We'd be driving for days through countryside and villages where there aren't any hotels as business people did not exist and nobody took holidays. I hated that idea and Mischa's exuberant mood got slightly on my nerves. I let him drive.

We travelled nonstop, driving past Vienna, and turned towards Czechoslovakia. It was weird. We hardly noticed the beauty of the countryside around us, the full blossoms of all the flowers, the bright green grass of the meadows as we were hurrying along the motorways.

We slept one night in a village in Czechoslovakia, in a communist type of hotel, eating horrid food for dinner but a great breakfast. After breakfast we sped on. At the border to Ukraine we stopped again, sitting down on the banks of the Dnieper river, overlooking fields and a village. I turned to Mischa.

'Do you know what? I'd like to go and see the place where I got shot. Where that girl got raped and I killed Moser.'

Mischa looked at me from the side, puffing a cigar.

'I was wondering whether you could face going there.'

'Definitely. The only problem is, I have no clue where it is...'

Mischa opened his rucksack and took out a map. He turned it around, looking for something. Then he pointed his finger to a spot that was circled with red ink.

'There.'

I looked at it.

'You're amazing, Mischa.'

'We could be there in two- or three-days' time, depending on the conditions of the roads.'

Mischa continued puffing his cigar, lying back in the grass. I lit my pipe and looked at the clouds that were floating west. I was thinking about Chernobyl, which had happened only four years earlier. Probably the grass we were sitting on was still contaminated.

We drove for three more days through lush countryside. Mischa loved the place, even though some forty-six years later, the road had not become an autobahn but was basically a badly asphalted mud-strip leading through forests, past rivers, lakes and green fields. We passed many small villages where many houses had not lost their pre-communist charm and looked like out of a Tolstoy novel rather than Brezhnev's Soviet Union. Surprisingly, they had survived the war. We watched kids playing football outside a beautiful wooden school house. Mischa decided to join in and kicked with the boys whilst I walked around the building and peeked through the windows. It seemed a happy place with lots of paintings and drawings on the walls and next to a photo of Comrade Gorbachev hung an old photo of Andropov.

Mischa continued to kick with the kids but then returned to the car, looking for something. He opened all the doors and then music came from the stereo. Beatles. *Back in the USSR*. I could not believe my ears.

We continued down the road whilst Mischa sang along. 'You don't know how lucky you are, boy.'

My mood was more sombre as we were soon reaching the spot where Mischa thought the place had been. Every time we passed some houses, I was wondering whether I'd recognise them. Mischa slowed down and looked around.

'There.'

'What do you mean?' I said, following Mischa's glance.

'Look at the lake on the left. That's the lake.' We stopped, left the Jeep at the roadside and climbed down to the lake. It looked the same, though memories can be deceiving after so many years.

I put my hand into the water in which I had swum almost half a century ago. It was cold and I realised suddenly that now it was May rather than summer. The water was clear and I quickly took off my clothes and jumped in. I dived deep. Here we had been, diving deep in the same lake. Feeling the endless peace underneath the water's surface.

Oleg Matjuchin

When I came back up, Mischa was already returning to the Jeep. I climbed up the bank and joined him.

'So refreshing and so pure.' I looked around. 'It's as if time had come to a complete standstill some fifty years ago.'

'Well, thank God it didn't. Let's go. We are almost there.'

We set off again to drive the short distance to the houses where Müller had shot me.

Mischa slowed down.

'Looks like this may be it,' he said, glancing at some buildings.

'No way, Mischa, they are post-war.'

'But it was here,' he insisted.

'Maybe.'

We got out of the car and looked around. The houses were shabby, Soviet style, without the charm of the other older houses we had been passing. Cheap with dirty windows, paint peeling off, the roofs badly repaired. We turned to the first one, which looked inhabited, its garden full of junk, collected over the years, buckets, bricks, wires, a window frame. The door was shut and we were unsure of what to do. A nameplate read "Matjuchin".

'Let's just knock and see who's there,' Mischa said.

For years I had nightmares about the event I had witnessed here. The screaming girl, the murdered Russian women on the ground, covered in blood, their brains spilling out on the floor. I always dreamed that I wanted to shoot but that my gun was jammed. That instead, they continued raping the girl, one after the other and, when they saw me, they started laughing their hoarse laughter, pulled their guns and both shot me. Sometimes in my dreams I saw the girl, saw her eyes staring at me, pleading to kill. I often wondered what had happened to her.

'Most likely, she was shot when they found Moser and Müller,' Mischa said, when I asked him the question. 'They probably shot her, burned the house, shot everyone in the next village and burned that one too.' Mischa looked at me sighing.

He knocked but nothing happened. We decided to wait by the car and lay down in the grass. I was awoken when I felt someone pushing against my foot. I looked up and saw an elderly man. It had gotten dark. He was thin with a sunk-in face, white hair and a slight hunchback.

'Good afternoon,' I said in Russian.

He stared at us with big and naïve eyes. 'Good afternoon. How can I help you?'

There was something about him which we could not understand, he looked slightly dazed as if he, not we, had woken up out of a dream.

'I'm Max Hardenberg and this is my friend Mischa,' I said.

'What? I don't hear well.'

I repeated myself, shouting. He nodded.

My Russian was still pretty good. Years in prisoner of war camp had given me a rudimentary layer of rough language, upon which I had later built the language of Pushkin and Chekhov at university and with Lena my Russian teacher.

'We're here on holiday, travelling around. Can we get some water for our Jeep? And a sip for ourselves, please.' Again, I had to shout to be understood.

'Oleg.' He stretched out his hand and we both shook it. 'Oleg Ivanovitch.' His grip was surprisingly firm. Oleg looked past us at the car with an expressionless face and then beckoned us to follow him into the house.

We entered the house. It consisted of a smallish living room with a sofa, four chairs, a dining table, an adjoining kitchen which looked like belonging to the previous century. Surprisingly, there was a beautiful abstract oil painting on the wall, next to the photo of comrade Brezhnev, like a time warp.

He indicated to us to sit down and we went over to the table and sat down on wooden chairs.

'I love it. So authentic,' Mischa whispered, taking in the details. Mischa spoke no Russian so I had to translate. Oleg came back with a jug and three glasses and poured us all some water.

'Well, what a surprise,' he said. 'We don't get many visitors over here.'

I took a sip from the glass, looking into the water, which tasted fresh and cool.

'From my own well,' he said.

There was silence.

'It's very beautiful over here,' I tried to start a conversation, but Oleg just looked at the table without moving. We sat in silence for a while.

'Beautiful house,' I said.

'Born here. Living here for a long time. But this one is new. Germans burned down the old one. Fuck the Germans.'

I translated.

'War is long over, and a lot has happened since. But I never forgive the Germans.' He looked out and then went into the garden, indicating to us that we should follow. 'See this road? Here they came by...tanks, tracks.' He did not seem to notice our number plate. He walked out of the garden on to the road. We followed him, slowly walking down the road.

'But one evening, I got back. I was a kid. And I saw two German Jeeps. And soldiers running around. A German soldier on a stretcher. And then another German soldier, on a stretcher. I was hiding there in the forest behind those trees.'

He stopped, looking at the trees, shaking his head. 'Those trees.'

He paused and stared at the trees with a blank expression. 'Then they burnt the house. I watched. Fuck the Germans.' He stood staring into the fading evening light.

'That's horrible,' I tried to say, but he did not seem to hear me.

'My sister Natasha wasn't in. But Mum dead. Babushka dead. Killed.'

'I'm sorry,' I said.

'Natasha ran away,' Oleg continued, looking down. 'Ran to Moscow.'

'And your father?'

'Shot by the political commissar. Dad hated Stalin.'

He was quiet for a moment and then turned to us, shrugging his shoulders.

'See? No difference. Fuck the Commissars and fuck the Germans.'

I saw that Mischa just wanted to get out of there but I wanted to find out the address of Natasha, his sister. Would he give it to us? I was hoping he would not find out where we were from before he had given it to us.

We returned to his living room. He took out a bottle of vodka and poured each of us a glass. I gulped down mine.

'Is your sister still alive?'

'Yes. In Moscow.'

We sat in silence as he stared at the wall for a while shaking his head as if answering silent questions.

'Never returned home,' he said eventually. Now it was his turn to gulp down his glass of vodka. Once he had refilled our glasses, he took another long sip before continuing.

'Really missed her but hated her. Never saw her again. And then, one day, her granddaughter came. Painted the blue painting. And left again.'

He looked for a long time at the painting and I saw

tears coming out of his eyes. He got up and went into the garden to the pump and pumped water into the jug and gave it to us to refill the car. It was dark outside. Mischa and I walked to the Jeep in silence, filled up the water and returned. When we got back to the house, Oleg was staring at the painting, the vodka bottle almost empty.

'Xenia,' he said, words slurred. 'Painted it. And left again. Don't know why.'

'It's very beautiful. I like it.'

He poured himself more vodka. I was not sure whether I could ask him about Natasha or whether he would be willing to help, but figured it was my only chance of finding out her address.

'Oleg,' I said, 'do you happen to have your sister's address in Moscow?'

'Ulitsa Petrova 16, fifth floor,' he said. 'I know it by heart. Never been.'

'Thank you.'

He opened another bottle of vodka and refilled our glasses. 'Never been.'

We gulped them down. The vodka was biting and calming.

'We need to go, Oleg,' I said.

He nodded. 'Where are you from?'

'Germany, Oleg.'

'Fuck the Germans,' he said expressionless.

'Here. Have one last shot.'

We gulped down yet another glass of vodka. 'You're OK,' he said. 'German. But OK. Fuck the other Germans.'

We thanked him and shook his hand and left him sitting in stupor on his chair. When we got out, we could hardly walk, we felt so drunk. We got into the car and drove a mile and stopped. Within minutes we had fallen asleep on our seats.

Volgograd

We drove casually for the next four days, stopping in villages, sleeping for hours in the sunshine, swimming in lakes that were cool and fresh. Most villages had no restaurants, just a collection of houses, sometimes a post office. We knocked at the doors and asked the farmers whether we could buy a meal and in most cases were invited in. People were so friendly even though they knew where we were from. I loved the simple food and vodka. After lunch we were mostly too drunk to drive on and slept somewhere on the roadside in the grass. Finally, we arrived in Volgograd. Mischa couldn't recognise anything. The last time he had been there, the town had already been destroyed. Bombed to pieces, no building had survived the onslaught, only skeletons of former houses had been left.

'We eradicated Stalingrad,' he said. 'Wiped it out... and now?' he looked around with astonished eyes. We parked the car in a small street and started walking towards the centre of town. Now Volgograd was a thriving city, busy, green, with friendly people, hurrying about. We went across town to the Volga. He remembered the river, sitting one day on its banks, a short while before the German army got encircled and most troops, who didn't die, got captured. Mischa had been away from his battalion when Field Marshal Paulus' army was destroyed.

Mischa had hated Stalingrad more than anything else. The fighting had been immensely vicious. House after house. He had told me the stories many times, both then and when we met in later years. 'We cleared a house, took it, moved on to the next, took it, got ambushed, had to retrench, retrench again, then forward again. Our comrades falling left, right and centre. I don't know how we survived. Or rather, why we survived.' He said it again as we were walking back to the main street, looking at the shops and the people rushing about. I never asked him whether he dreamt about this. We never spoke about dreams.

We stayed for three days, sightseeing, drinking tea, walking around aimlessly, visiting the museum and the statue of Mother Rodina, a huge sculpture on the hill slightly outside town. The town still had a Soviet feel to it. People were wearing typical communist style clothes, lacking any elegance and going shopping was a typical communist experience, showing how people were generally mistrusted: first you queue to see what you want to buy and how much it would cost, then, next, you have to join a different queue at the till and pay the amount and get a receipt, with the receipt you queue again to pick up what you wanted to buy. Shopping was tedious as there were shortages of everything except cabbage – and queues. But we loved sitting in the many little cafés you find in town, eating ice cream, which you buy not in scoops but in lots of fifty or a hundred grams. We normally ate three-hundred grams in one go and felt very flash and nouveau riche about it. Often people joined us at our table and started talking to us – it was pretty obvious that we were foreigners. To our surprise, they were not shy and hostile, but friendly, open and welcoming. No one else seemed to think, 'Fuck the Germans'.

'Surprising that none of them shows any bitterness about the war,' Mischa observed. No justice had been done and yet their arms were open and their smiles were genuine. Mischa had no answer either.

'You know, it's weird, but I feel somewhat guilty,' I said. 'We are eating tons of ice cream when they can hardly afford bloody cabbage.'

We went to buy our 300 grams of ice cream nonetheless and looked around for an empty table. As there was none, we asked a couple whether we could join them. 'Of course, you can. Where are you from?'

'Germany,' Mischa said.

'Woww. I love Germany. Great technology,' the man said.

It turned out he was an engineer from Volgograd and his wife was a soprano at the opera house.

'Have you been to the opera?' She asked, and when we indicated no, she immediately invited us for the next day.

'I'll send you two tickets,' she said when they got up to leave.

The next morning at breakfast in the hotel, the receptionist handed us an envelope with two tickets for the evening's performance of Evgeny Onegin.

'Evgeny who?' I asked Mischa.

'You bloody peasant. It's Tchaikovsky. Based on Pushkin. Bet you have not heard of him either.'

'Not lawyers.'

'Shit, Max, definitely not.'

The opera house was amazing. In neo-baroque style. I spotted our new friend, beautifully dressed, singing beautifully. I had to admit, the singing was good but what was charming was that members of the orchestra each had a big jug of beer standing next to their chairs and were happily drinking away when they were not playing.

Our host from last night had brought his father along. The old gentleman was wearing a jacket with a whole array of military decorations.

'He was a Colonel during the war,' explained his son. 'Now he's 85 and can hardly walk or speak.' He turned to his father. 'These are friends from Germany,' he said. The colonel held out his hand and just smiled without saying anything. We shook his hand, moved by the warmth of his welcome. 'He fought in Volgograd and was part of the brigade that closed the circle, trapping the German army. He is immensely proud of it.'

'He should be,' I said.

'Yes, he is strange. On the one hand he still lives in the past wearing all his decorations, on the other hand, he likes the Germans and told me this morning he wanted to meet you and see you with his own eyes.'

'Has he not seen any Germans since the war?'

'No, he has, of course. There have been German students studying Russian in the summer at our uni and he always goes to meet them. Seems to like them, particularly the girls.'

In the break we treated our hosts to Champanskoye and caviar. Delicious Champanskoye but I hated the caviar. The Colonel stuck to vodka.

In the evening of the third day, Mischa looked for a public phone at the post office to call his wife Helena. Whilst we were walking around Volgograd, he had told me that he had gone for a full medical check-up at a clinic in Stuttgart the other day, a thing neither he nor I had ever contemplated before as we both considered ourselves basically healthy. 'Why did you do this?'

'Got persuaded by a friend of Helena's and was simply curious.'

'About what? I'm not curious about my health. If I'm ill, I'll know soon enough.'

I sat down on a bench whilst he was on the phone. Ten minutes later he returned. From the look on his face I knew that something was not right. His wife had sounded worried, he explained. The hospital suspected cancer and Helena urged him to come home immediately.

I looked at him and didn't know what to say and searched for my pipe instead.

'I don't know Max, I mean, I don't feel bad; OK, I don't have the energy I used to have, but that's age, isn't it? I just don't feel as if I have cancer.' He looked around and then got up and walked towards the car.

'Hey, let's at least enjoy something unhealthy, in the

meantime.' He got out two cigars and I decided to join him, sensing that this would be our last day together in the USSR. We went to a café and sat down, ordering chai and started smoking. I looked at Mischa. He seemed healthy, he had this twinkle in his eyes, as if he were still a little boy.

'You'll be OK', I said after a while. 'Cancer can be treated today much better than twenty years ago, and you're a fighter, Mischa, you'll be fine.'

He continued puffing his cigar, but then said after a while, 'I'm not terribly worried, Max, but I think I'd still like to go back and get more tests done and start treatment if that's indeed needed.'

We decided that he should fly back the next day, taking a domestic flight from Volgograd to Moscow and I would drive back alone, once I had seen enough of town.

Moscow

The next day the airport was full of farmers checking in huge bags of vegetables and I believe even chickens to fly to Moscow to sell all on the local market. I watched as Mischa's slightly dilapidated Aeroflot Tupolev took off and slowly disappeared into the sky. I drove back into town and walked around alone. The place was suddenly lonely and lacking charm. I missed Mischa. It seemed so unfair.

The following morning I got into the Jeep and decided to drive to Moscow instead of going back home.

It took me two and a half days to cover the 600 miles. I took it easy, stopping in little villages, at kolkhoz farms, enjoying fresh milk in the mornings and tea and vodka in the afternoons. Everywhere I went, people were poor but friendly and curious. Both evenings, I got invited to dinner and joined the farmers around their table, drinking vodka and eating rough, delicious bread with butter and cheese, or thick vegetable soup. I woke up both mornings and found the simple table in the kitchen prepared with eggs, milk and wonderfully brown but tasteless instant coffee.

In the end I arrived in Moscow, late in the afternoon and decided to stay at the Gostinitsa Rossia. A monumental hotel with three thousand rooms, miles of corridors, restaurants, bars, and even a prison. A young bell-boy took me up to my room which was a lot bigger than the usual 11 square metres. I looked out on to the street which was busy underneath me. It all still smelled and looked of communism. I unpacked and decided to walk a bit, across Red Square. The square was relatively empty, a few tourists, no queue in front of Lenin's Mausoleum. I decided to enter the GUM instead. It was not Harrods or the KaDeWe. The choice of goods was pathetic in this, Moscow's most important, shopping mall. I quickly left again and felt like doing all those things instead that I never did in Munich, like going to museums, to concerts, to the opera, watching the Bolshoi Ballet. In the Arbat quarters I bought a CD of Russian music, Bulat Okudshava, Mischa's favourite. Later, I called Mischa, but he had no news.

I hesitated about going to see Natasha. All of a sudden, I was not sure anymore what to say. Instead I went to the Tretyakov Gallery which was totally empty except for a group of schoolchildren who were sitting in front of some medieval icons, trying to draw Jesus and Mary. I preferred the section with Soviet art instead.

Finally, on my fourth day, I went to Ulitsa Petrova 16. It was strange how Igor had immediately told me the exact address when I asked him, even though he had never been. What was going on in his head? Damage from the war, and yet not attributed to the war.

During the last two days my hesitation had turned into the need to meet Natasha. Something was dragging me there. A mix of confusion and curiosity. Over all those years I had been thinking about her, more than about other things that happened during the war, more than about other horrors I had witnessed as her silhouette and her screams had for ever been ingrained in my memory. And because I felt guilty for not having killed Müller, the other SS swine. I felt I could close a chapter and calm down if I could talk to her, see her, hold her hands and apologise.

I looked around, a typical Soviet style apartment building, set into suburbia amongst other typical Soviet style apartment buildings: ugly, functional, a narrow staircase, grey walls with paint peeling off where ever there was paint. Concrete charm except for the beautiful birch trees that grew in front of the house. In the distance, I heard someone practicing the violin – badly. I climbed up to the fifth floor, almost bumping into kids who came rushing down, and rang the bell.

After some time I heard footsteps and the door opened. A woman in her sixties looked at me slightly surprised.

'Natasha Ivanovna?'

'Yes.' She looked at me with suspicion. 'What do you want?'

'Your brother Oleg gave me your address,' I continued, realising the moment I said it that the mere mentioning of her brother might close the door for me for good. She stood transfixed and looked at me with sharp eyes.

'My brother, you said?'

'Yes, Oleg Ivanovitch Matjuchin. I met him last week at his house.'

I realised suddenly I did not even know the name of

the nearby village or of that lake. Neither had I introduced myself. 'My name is Max Hardenberg,' I added. We shook hands, while she observed me sceptically.

'Well, come on in, rather than talking in the doorframe,' she said reluctantly, stepping back. I entered her apartment. It was smallish, a hallway with three doors at the end, a kitchen, a living room, into which she led me. She pulled a chair towards the table and offered it to me. I sat down. She took two glasses out of the cupboard and turned to me, 'would you like some tea?'

A samovar was standing in the corner and Natasha filled the two glasses with dark tea.

'What were you doing visiting my brother?' She eyed me suspiciously. I paused, looking into the glass of chai as if searching for an answer, stirring the sugar until it had dissolved. It tasted sweet and bitter. I realised, I wasn't quite sure how to explain why I had come to visit her. So I was glad that she asked the question first.

'I was travelling with a friend of mine. We are both from Germany. We were on our way to visit Volgograd.'

'That's a long trip,' she said and I noticed for the first time a faint smile.

'It's actually a long story,' I said apologetically.

Natasha leant back in her chair, now more relaxed. Then she glanced at me inquisitively. I decided I needed to tell her the whole story now, otherwise I would never have a second chance.

'Let me take a step back,' I started again. 'I used to be a judge and lived in Munich. But before, I mean during the war I was a child. At least at the beginning. Then I got drafted in 1943 and had to go to the front.' I paused, studying her reaction. But her face did not reveal any emotions, so I continued. 'I ended up in Ukraine and then as a prisoner of war in Russia. That's where I learned to speak your language.'

'You do speak it well,' she said.

'Thank you. I've forgotten a lot though. But five years in camp teaches you the basics.'

She looked at me from the side and poured some more tea.

'But before I got captured, I once got wounded. It happened one afternoon. We were coming back from a swim in a lake and we got to a house and saw a Jeep parked in front of it. We didn't know who it was, except that it was clear – the Jeep belonged to the SS.'

Again, I paused, observing her face. She was concentrating on the tea, studying the leaves, stirring them with her spoon. I took some more sugar and put it into mine, stirring, before continuing. Natasha got up and went over to the bookshelf, as if looking for something.

'Do continue, please,' she said, looking over her shoulder.

'For some reason, we were drawn towards the house. I perched myself up to the window and, looking through it, was horrified by what I saw. Two SS officers. It was horrible. Somewhat instinctively I pulled my gun and shot one of them. I think I killed him instantly. But by the time I was aiming at the second he had already pulled his gun.

We fired at the same time. I got him but he hit me too. I wanted to shoot again but fainted and collapsed. This happened at your brother's house.'

Natasha had turned around and sat down again. Looking into her glass, and then at me, she shook her head.

'I was taken to a field hospital. Our captain drove me there. He still saw a girl running away. I... I don't know. I fainted and only woke up in the hospital.'

It was strange. I felt a bewildering sense of relief once I had told her the story. I looked at my hand, which was shaking, spilling the tea. I could not move in my chair and looked at her, afraid of her reaction.

There was a long pause and Natasha got up, walked over to the window and looked out.

'So it was you,' she said quietly. 'For years I wasn't sure who had shot those bastards. I wanted to believe that it was one of our comrades, but there was the officer who came in after the shooting. He checked things, looked at me, and walked out again. It all didn't make any sense as he was German. I thought he was going to kill me too. First, I was paralysed with fear but then I panicked and ran away as I feared he might rape me as well. I was more afraid of being raped again than of being killed.' She paused a moment and then said, 'So it was you who came into the house?'

'No. I was lying on the floor outside the window with a bullet in my shoulder. Couldn't move. It was my friend Mischa.'

'And you said you shot the two Nazi officers?'

'Yes, I did.'

'I haven't spoken about this to anyone for ages. I just wanted to bury the past and get on with life. But I'm so shocked and amazed to see you here.'

There was another pause and she got up again, depositing her tea cup into the sink. 'You have to excuse me for a minute.' She walked into the corridor and left me alone in the room, closing the door behind her.

I got up and looked down into the courtyard where kids were playing football. In the dreary house across a woman was hanging up laundry. I felt as if a huge burden had been lifted off my chest but then again, I thought about Natasha's face, her restrained initial reaction and then her sudden exit. Why was I doing this? Should I not had left her in peace? What peace? Was I just incredibly egotistical by trying to come to grips with my own past? In a way, I was surprised about myself too. I had not talked about the war with many people. Except with Mischa. And yet, it had been disturbing me all those years, I now have to admit. Yes, I needed to apologise to Natasha to come to a closure, to find peace myself. All of a sudden, I noticed that tears were running down my cheeks. These memories were overpowering. I took the handkerchief to dry my face and poured myself more tea, to calm down.

It felt like hours till Natasha came back.

'I am sorry,' she said. 'This is just too much for me.'

I got up, but she hurriedly said, 'No, please don't go. I need to talk about this now that you are here, please.' We both sat down again and she continued.

'When you saw me coming out of our house, I just ran away. Ran and ran and ran, what seemed day and night, till I had reached my auntie's house. That I didn't get caught by some Germans is a miracle. I first stayed with my aunt. A week after I arrived, the news reached us that the Germans had burned our house down and that everyone in there was dead. I thought that my brother was dead too.' She got up again but continued after a while, having searched her cupboards for something.

'Then I realised that I was pregnant,' she said. 'I was so disgusted with myself. I wanted to terminate this pregnancy but couldn't find anyone to perform the abortion. I was so desperate. In the end, I found a doctor in the next town. I don't recall how I managed to get there, considering that the Nazis were everywhere. But I did. It was strange, though, as by the time I had found him, I couldn't go through with it anymore. It was, as if my child cried to me: "Don't kill me." It was as if I'd gone mad – I could hear this little voice in my dreams but then also during the day. I banged my head against walls, but it didn't help.' She stopped.

'And so I didn't have an abortion. Instead I moved to Moscow straight after we were liberated and raised the child. It was a girl. I called her Olga. I loved her so much.'

I had to press my lips tightly together to suppress my tears and that rising feeling of anger and bitterness. I could not speak and looked at her face and saw that she again had tears in her eyes. I had no handkerchief to offer her. Natasha took her sleeve and wiped her face.

'So, why did you want to visit me?'

'I felt I was missing something. All those years, I felt guilty about what had happened, guilty that I had not protected you. I had these pictures of you in my head, of you running out of the house. I wanted to hear what had happened to you.' I paused and then added: 'And I wanted to apologise for what we had done.'

'But it wasn't you,' Natasha said, looking at me. 'You don't need to apologise.' Her face was serious. 'And now you see that I actually am alright,' she said. 'I'm actually fine. I love my life here in Moscow, where I'm free,' she said with a sigh.

'No, you may not understand, but I do need to apologise. I feel guilty for what we have done. We. The Germans.'

She looked away and we both drank our tea in silence.

'And does Olga live in Moscow too? She must be 45 by now, I guess.'

'She would have been,' Natasha said. 'But, no, she died. In fact, she committed suicide.' She corrected herself with a calm voice.

I looked at her and tried to see the emotions showing on her face.

'She killed herself years ago. She had a daughter herself, who was six when it happened.' She paused, searching for words. 'It was very sad then, but now I've got over things. And Xenia, Olga's daughter, became such a happy grandchild, despite losing her mother so early in life.' She paused again.

'Olga never managed to accept herself. She hated herself. From the moment she found out that her father was an SS officer, she despised herself and could not get over that fact. It was a painful burden for her that half of her came from an SS rapist and only the other half was normal. She often said that she would like to get rid of her SS half so that she'd become pure and clean. She could not appreciate the fact that she was hundred per cent innocent in this world. It became an obsession, I don't know. She told me she wanted to kill herself, but I didn't believe her. Nobody believed her, but in the end she did. And by then it was too late.'

'I'm sorry.'

I felt somewhat cheap the moment I was saying this. Light words in contrast to the heaviness of her story. Outside, evening had come and the sun cast long shadows in the courtyard. Natasha got up and got herself a packet of cigarettes. She offered one to me and, when I refused, she lit one using the matches on her kitchen stove.

'Olga never got married. She had flings with a number of men. Writers, painters, circus artists, then a Soviet bureaucrat. Then a black student who was studying engineering here in Moscow. Well, I know for certain that the baby wasn't from him. But she never told me who the father was and none of her boyfriends ever claimed responsibility. In fact, as soon as she had got visibly pregnant, they all disappeared out of her life. The painter is the only one I quite liked. Victor. I loved his colours.'

She got up and beckoned me to follow.

'Here. Have a look. I have one of his paintings in the next room.'

I followed her down the corridor into a room. It was small and dark, a bed, a desk, shelves full of books, the window facing the dirty wall of the house opposite hers. And a piano. The painting was hanging over it. I hesitated. It was an oil painting, abstract, with powerful colours.

'This is Xenia's room.' There were more paintings standing against the wall.

'Xenia did those. She paints from time to time.'

'And plays the piano?'

Natasha nodded.

'No longer this one, though. She played it when she was much younger. Now she only practices at the conservatory,' she said with obvious pride.

'So she is studying music?'

'Yes. The piano and composition.'

'That's wonderful. I'm impressed.'

I went to have a closer look at her paintings. Big canvasses with broad brushstrokes and mainly primary colours: white, blue, red, yellow. All abstract and quite similar to the one on Oleg's wall.

'I must say, I like them. Even more than the one on the wall. I like the colours and composition.'

She turned to leave the room whilst I had a last look around. 'I'm sorry, but I have to go now. I'm working late shifts at the factory this week, and mine starts soon. So I need to leave in about ten minutes.'

'May I accompany you to work?' I offered.

'No. No thanks. I am OK. It's pretty close by anyway,' she said, shaking her head. 'But I would like to see you again, if that's OK with you. On Sunday I have my day off and maybe Xenia will be around too. We could all go…'

'Let me treat you both to lunch,' I interrupted. 'Please do ask Xenia to join us too.'

'Oh, that's very kind of you, I think she'd be pleased.'

We parted at the bus stop, having agreed that I would pick them up at eleven from their place. Trolleybuses are something typical of Moscow. Bulat Okudshava even composed a song about the midnight trolleybus.

I headed back towards town, feeling angry and shameful, yes, and bitter. Even though I did apologise, I felt that my apology was trite, that it was not enough. It suddenly struck me: there had been no justice and even though Natasha was leading a normal life, the pain remained raw underneath a thin surface. And yet I did not know what to do. I could not simply drive back to Munich and leave things now that I had opened this Pandora's box. Somehow, I sensed that her granddaughter Xenia might help me, and her, close this chapter. But I did not know how.

Xenia's paintings came back into my mind, the colours, the brushstrokes. I tried to think what type of person she might be. Her paintings were vibrant, almost aggressive – what would she be like? I could not imagine her to be much like Natasha. But can one judge a painter by his or her paintings? Was Rothko as serene as his paintings indicated or Pollock as chaotic? Crossing the river Moskva

I sat down on a bench and observed the crowd walking past. I lit my pipe. I loved the mellow taste of pipe tobacco. Moscow is similarly mellow. So is Russian music, Russian wine. Only vodka isn't mellow.

Sunday was a beautiful day, sunny, warm with a light wind. I woke up early, feeling nervous about our second meeting. What would Natasha be like today, now that she had time to reflect? What would Xenia say? How much did she know?

I had breakfast at the hotel and took the Jeep to drive around town, eventually heading out towards the suburbs to arrive at Natasha's place just before eleven o'clock. I walked up and rang the bell. A girl opened with a smile.

'Welcome. You must be Max. Do come in. Babka's just stepped out, she'll be back any minute.'

I hesitated and she stretched out her hand. 'I'm Xenia, by the way,' she said, smiling.

I briefly looked at her thin hand observing her long fingers. She had a very firm grip. All the while, she continued looking into my eyes, which threw me slightly off balance. What had Natasha told her about me?

'Would you like some tea whilst we're waiting?' she said as we entered the kitchen. Without waiting for my answer, she poured me a glass of tea and put it on to the table, sitting down opposite me.

'So you're the pianist?' I said.

'Yes, how do you know?'

'Well, your grandmother told me so. She's very proud of you.'

'She thinks I'm great, but I am actually crap,' she said disarmingly.

I looked at her to see whether she was coy or joking. For some reason I sensed that she might not be as bad as she pretended to be.

'Well, was Richter famous at your age?'

'I didn't start giving concerts when I was ten.'

I had to laugh. 'You really are super ambitious. Why don't you just enjoy your studies and then see what happens.'

'I guess you're right,' she said. 'But I don't want to end up as some crappy piano teacher in the fucking suburbs. No perspective whatsoever. Like our neighbour across the yard. No, you know, when you're my age, you should be allowed to dream.'

She took a sip of tea from her cup, holding it delicately with her right hand.

'So, once you reach my age, ambitions are basically gone?'

'Depends on how old you are,' she said innocently. 'Anything over fifty is bad news.'

Again she laughed and I looked at her eyes and then it struck me what was remarkable about them: They were green. Not blue or grey with some touch of green, but really green, a sort of emerald green. I was stunned.

I didn't know what to answer anymore. This was the clumsiest small talk I'd ever had. Bang. Anything over fifty is bad news. I thought Germans were pretty direct, but she was a T34 tank.

At that moment the door opened and Natasha entered.

'So, welcome back, Max. Sorry I'm late.' She came over and shook my hand.

'I'm very glad to see you again Natasha,' I said.

'I hope Xenia kept you entertained.'

'Amused,' I said.

'Xenia?' Natasha said, glancing over to her granddaughter. 'She was absolutely charming. But, let's get going. I've made a reservation at the Dom Literaturov in town.'

'Brilliant. I love that place,' Xenia said, jumping up.

'You know it?' Her grandmother said.

'Sure. I used to hang out there with Andrei and Sasha.'

'Too intellectual for me,' Natasha said.

We set off in the Jeep and arrived in the back street behind the restaurant some thirty minutes later. It turned out that Xenia had never been in a Jeep and absolutely loved the experience. How weird for an artist to be interested in Jeeps.

We entered the restaurant, which was still relatively empty. It had a warm and welcoming atmosphere.

'It's funny. Foreigners always want to eat borscht, as if that's the only thing we can cook in Russia,' Natasha said when I had ordered.

'Oh, come on Babka,' Xenia interrupted. 'Russian food sucks.'

'But it's good. I love it. It's much better than German food,' I said.

'Oh,' Xenia quickly said, 'that's easy, isn't it?'

'Xenia, please.'

'What is it, Babka?' she said innocently. 'German and Russian food is like our literature: Just bloody heavy.'

'That's probably true,' I said.

We ate in silence, Natasha observing both of us.

'So, tell me, Max, what do you read?' Xenia said.

I had to think as literature was not really my great strength. In the evenings I was much happier with a book on criminal law, a thriller where the good guy wins in the end, or even a comic strip rather than Thomas Mann or Herman Hesse.

'Max Frisch is my favourite,' I answered cautiously.

'Which of his books?' Xenia said.

I loved *Homo Faber* and *Montauk*. *Montauk* always reminded me of a conference I went to in New York. I read the novel on the plane, and felt sadness coming over me. Memories. I remember closing the book once I had finished the last page and drinking three glasses of cognac till we landed in New York. The next morning I skipped the conference and rented a car instead and drove out to Montauk. It was in the autumn and the leaves were turning gold, an Indian summer. I had a cassette of Joe Dassin and played *L'été Indien* over and over. I was thinking of Julia who I had loved so much and lost. I was crying. I put the music on full blast and drove on till I reached the beach. Taking off my shoes, I walked on the fine sand, the music still in my ears along with the waves on the empty beach. I only gradually stopped crying as the sun was setting. Finally, I thought,

Julia's death was hitting me full blast in the stomach after all those years. I had cried at her funeral but immediately buried myself in work in order not to have to think. And now it had hit me. Way after midnight, in total darkness, I walked back to the car and drove to Manhattan.

I looked up. Both Natasha and Xenia were waiting patiently.

'Sorry,' I said. 'Actually, being a judge, I prefer Dürrenmatt. Absolutely wonderful thrillers. Great for lawyers.'

'Hmm,' Xenia reflected. 'Dark sense of humour. So unlike the Swiss.'

'Let me ask you,' I changed the topic. 'Who's your favourite composer?'

'Definitely Schumann and Rachmaninoff. And Beethoven. But I also like Chopin.'

'Hmm. That's more than one.'

'Yes, I like more than one.'

'Sonatas or concertos?'

'Concertos of course. Both Schumann and Rachmaninoff are totally amazing. Very different, but deep, melancholic deep. Joyful. Don't know. A bit like chocolate fondant. They must have been totally screwed up.'

She paused to think.

'And are you giving any concerts nowadays?'

'Of course she is,' Natasha said proudly. 'I've heard her twice already.'

'Recitals or orchestra?'

'Orchestra,' Xenia said, chewing her food. 'I've played

with the Moscow Radio Orchestra and also in Kiev and Volgograd.'

'And you said you were really bad.' I paused. 'I have a different idea of *really bad*.'

'Yeah, but always Schumann. Just bloody Schumann. No one wants to listen to me playing Rachmaninoff.'

'But that's pretty good. You haven't even finished the Conservatory and you are already giving concerts.'

'I'm a bloody one Schumann trick pony.'

She stopped and, looking at her plate, started poking with her fork at the food. Something seemed to have changed, although I had felt all along that there was something in the air, something not quite right.

'But tell me, Max,' she said, hesitating, 'where do you and Babka know each other from. I couldn't get a word out of her, so you must explain. And, secondly, how come that you speak such good Russian, too well for a German?'

'Well,' Natasha quickly interjected, 'Max was travelling around and just came from Volgograd.'

I nodded.

'Don't like the place,' Xenia said. 'I mean the Volga is nice and stuff, but the place has no face. No soul.' She paused and added after a moment, 'so, why would you go to Volgograd?'

'We drove all the way. Through Ukraine,' I said.

'Through Ukraine. Hmm. Why?'

'To get to Volgograd, you have to drive through Ukraine,' Natasha said.

'I know bloody Geography, Babka, thanks.'

Xenia became quiet, narrowing her eyes. Something seemed now to have definitely changed inside her and her happy mischievous eyes had turned cold and calculating.

I was not sure anymore whether Natasha had not told her grand-daughter our story. I looked at her, but Natasha seemed to raise her eyebrows, looking at the people across the room. I had to be truthful to Xenia, but did Xenia know the whole story?

'I wanted to go back and see the country in peacetime. I wanted to drive down the roads I had walked many years ago during the war.' I paused.

'And Max met with Oleg over there,' Natasha said with a quiet voice.

Xenia looked down at her food, pretending to pick up a piece of onion with her fork. There was a long silence and I observed her face. It was getting paler.

'Then, tell me, Max,' Xenia said, almost in a whisper. 'Tell me,' she paused, looking directly at me with cold and piercing eyes. 'It wasn't pure coincidence that you bumped into Babka's brother? And that he gave you Babka's address? And that you're visiting us? Right?'

Natasha turned away, looking at the neighbouring table, where an elderly couple had just sat down.

'No,' I said. 'I wanted to return.' I looked at Xenia. Her fist was clenched around her knife so that her knuckles were white. She was sitting rigid in her chair.

'No, Xenia. Please, let's not go over this again,' Natasha interjected.

'What?' Xenia hissed. 'I have a right to know, Babka.'

'There's no point in bringing things up again. It's over. Over.'

'No, Babka. Not for me,' she said with a quiet voice. 'Mum killed herself.'

She turned to me.

'Max. I want to know. Were you there when,' she paused and fixed me with icy eyes and whispered: 'you know what happened? Is that why you returned?'

'No, darling,' Natasha said turning around, putting her hand on to Xenia's arm. 'You've got it completely wrong, if that's what you're thinking: Max isn't...' she paused, searching for the right word and then swallowed, shaking her head. 'Do you really think I would be sitting here at the same table with him? How stupid do you think I am?'

'Babka, who the fuck is he then?' she hissed. 'Tell me.'

'Max,' Natasha paused for a moment, as if to recollect a thought and then looked at Xenia. 'Max killed him. Shot the guy,' again she paused, desperately avoiding saying the word to her grand-daughter. 'He killed him.'

I looked at Xenia. She slumped back into her chair, grabbing her glass of wine and taking a deep sip and then a second sip, finishing the glass. She got up and went towards the door but turned around again and came over to me. Bowing down, she took me into her arms from behind and hugged me for a long time. I was stunned and did not know what to do, feeling her tears running down her cheek on to mine. Quietly, she was sobbing. Finally she let go and walked over to the desk at the side of the room, took a napkin and cleaned her face. She remained standing, facing the wall, holding on to it as if for support. I looked around, but none of the other guests seemed to have noticed anything. After a while Xenia turned around and came back. She sat down and looked at me with watery eyes.

'I'm sorry, Max,' she paused, looking for words, 'I almost accused you of... I know, I shouldn't have. My thinking was totally fucked up. Don't know what came over me, I just couldn't think straight. What a fuckwit I am. And now I don't know what to say or how to thank you.'

'You don't need to thank me, Xenia,' I said. 'To the contrary, I feel bad about it. I arrived too late. I wish I could have shot them earlier.' We remained silent. I poured both Natasha and Xenia some more wine and finished my glass too. The wine was deep, heavy, ruby red and had an earthen melancholy taste.

'I wish Mum could be here and meet you. It would have helped her a lot, knowing that you killed that person who,' she hesitated for a while, thinking, and then said, 'who was that half of hers she hated so much.'

She sighed, shrugging her shoulders.

'But then again, life's moved on.'

She paused and looked at me first with a sad face, but then her expression changed. 'Had you been the rapist, I would have killed you right here in the restaurant. Holy fuck.' Again she paused, and then she added more relaxed, 'let's order desserts – I need something sweet and heavy now.'

I felt hugely relieved when I saw how Xenia had managed to change back, how she managed to talk again, minutes after almost killing me. I took a handkerchief and wiped the sweat off my forehead.

Xenia ordered mousse au chocolat, which even in Russia tastes wonderful, despite the lack of decent Suisse or Belgian chocolate. I needed it in order to calm down again. We ate the mousse in silence. From time to time Xenia looked at me, whilst I tried to concentrate on the molten chocolate.

When we got up, Natasha took my arm as we walked out of the restaurant. I think we all felt exhausted and needed time to think, but I also felt the urge to continue talking with Natasha and Xenia.

'I'll leave you here,' Natasha said. 'I need some time alone now.'

'Can I drive you home?'

'No, please don't worry. Honestly. This has been a bit much and I need time alone.'

'I can stay a bit longer, if you have time,' Xenia said looking at me.

'I'd like to see you again, though,' Natasha said.

'Yes, definitely, me too,' I replied.

'And thank you so much for lunch, Max.'

We hugged and she said goodbye to Xenia and turned around. Xenia and I remained standing outside the restaurant and watched her as she walked away. I felt sorry for Natasha, seeing her walking with her head down, burdened by the terrible past which she thought she had pushed away and which was now hitting her again. Again,

I felt a pang of guilt as it was me who had brought things up. But I also sensed that my appearance would finally allow her to overcome the past rather than just pushing it away. Eventually, when she was lost in the crowd, Xenia pulled me out of my thoughts. I looked at the buildings which had no charm left and was glad when we reached Arbat with its pre-revolutionary buildings that nowadays seemed to look melancholy and slightly frail. The afternoon sun gave Xenia's hair a dark glow. As we were walking, I looked at her from the side. Xenia was slim and her face had typical Slavic traits: high cheek bones, a petite nose, thin pale lips; her skin was relatively tanned. And then her eyes, the emerald green, which could be bright when she was full of joy or icy, even when she was trying to hide her anger. When we reached the busy crossing, we stopped and Xenia turned around. She looked into my eyes with a tender intensity.

'I never thanked anyone for killing another person. I don't think that killing is right. But I do thank you for killing who you killed.' She paused and then hugged me briefly.

I did not know what to say as I was overcome by emotions when I felt her embrace. I felt relieved when the traffic light turned green and we could cross the street. Xenia turned around and looked at me. She seemed so ascetic and yet tough. I had that strange feeling of being drawn towards her, which I could not understand or rationally explain. I think it had struck me the moment she had opened the door of her apartment. I don't normally have such feelings.

'Shall we take the Metro to the park?' Her words suddenly woke me out of my semi-hypnotized state. I realised I couldn't. I had to withdraw, this was getting too much. I could not simply walk around town with Natasha's granddaughter. What was I getting myself into?

I turned to her.

'That would be nice, Xenia,' I said. 'But I don't think I can make it. I need to call my friend Mischa today and I'm just not sure when he'll be at home.' We reached the Metro and walked down the stairs on to the platform.

'That's a shame,' she said with a glance that implied she was seeing straight through my lie. 'So I'll never see you again?'

'I don't know. I mean, I don't know when. I'd wanted to visit your grandmother again, and maybe you'll be there too.'

'Maybe.' Xenia glanced at me and we heard the rumble of the Metro from the distance in the tunnel.

'Look. On Tuesday I'll be at Leninskoje Gorje Metro station at three pm. I'll wait for ten minutes. You'll either be there, or you won't be there. Your choice.'

The Metro pulled into the station, the doors opened and people were coming out of the carriages. I did not know what to say and she quickly touched my shoulder with her hand, turned around and entered the carriage. 'Poka,' she said as the doors were closing.

I had a strange feeling in my stomach as the train started accelerating and pulled out of the station. I went back to the street and back to the Jeep and returned to the hotel. I had to lie down on my bed and drink a cognac to taste the bitter sweetness of the numbing liquid. It quietened me down. I had to think logically.

There was nothing wrong about having tea with Xenia in Moscow. Full stop. What was going on in my head? I was such an idiot, being shaken by the first woman who looked at me, who was kind to me, misinterpreting her kindness. And all of that, I realised, just because I had been a stupid hermit for the last decades, not loving anyone, refusing, and hence not being loved by anyone.

But should I turn up on Tuesday? Would it not be better to let that day simply pass by? I struggled, as deep inside I realised that Xenia had awakened something I did not know how to handle.

I forgot to call Mischa.

Tuesday

Monday passed by. I had to kill time and decided to drive around town, down the endless six lane avenues, lined with ugly skyscrapers. At five in the afternoon I went up to the Leninskoje Gorje, the big park, or, as the name says, the hills, stretching over and around the river Moskva, from where you have stunning views over the city. Having checked out the entrances to the Metro, I went back to the hotel and drank a bottle of wine from room service without eating anything and fell asleep before nine o'clock. The next morning I was nervous but it was too early to drink alcohol. At eleven I went to have lunch. At two I took the Metro to the Leninskoje Gorje.

I decided to sit down on a bench opposite the Metro entrance to observe people coming out. An old man came out, *Pravda* under his arm. He walked on. Two young women stopped at the entrance and lit a cigarette, chatting. No Xenia. I waited, looking at my watch. 20 seconds to go. A dog came out alone, looking for his owner, who followed shortly afterwards, but by then the dog had disappeared. The owner whistled as a clock struck three. Two hands came down on my shoulders from behind me. Xenia laughed.

'Scared?' She came around to stand in front of me

and looked at me all innocent. 'I knew you'd come.' She stretched out her hands to pull me up and kissed me on both cheeks. 'Let's go,' she said. 'There is a little place where we can have tea.'

We set off, walking along the paths, looking over the city towards the spires of the Kremlin walls, which allowed me to look at her again from the side, observing her beautiful silhouette. So here I was, walking in Moscow with Natasha's granddaughter on a sunny afternoon.

'Hey, wake up, Max,' Xenia nudged me, laughing. 'You're day-dreaming.'

We continued walking until we reached a café where we sat down, ordering chai and biscuits. I watched her as she delicately poured the tea into my cup. She looked at me and said innocently, 'Babka told me you're a judge?'

'Well, yes and no. I was a judge till recently. But I retired. So now I'm just free, living, enjoying life, thinking about what to do next.'

'Any ideas?'

'Not sure yet. I'm working on a legal paper right now.'

'Boring.'

'You know, when you live your life day in day out, when you enjoy what you do and when you don't do many other things besides your work, it's difficult to think about something completely new.'

'Long sentence. But no hobbies?'

'Not really.'

'So what did you do during your holidays?'

'Sorry. It's sort of weird. For years the only holidays

I took were holidays in Austria or Switzerland, going mountaineering, either alone or with a friend of mine.'

'Shit, that's boring. I love visiting cities.'

'I don't. Unless I can go to legal conferences.'

'Seaside?'

'I've not been to the sea, I mean, on holiday, just to lie on the beach.'

'Fuck, you are one-dimensional,' she laughed. 'And you never got bored with yourself?'

I had to swallow. She was right. I had become boring. A boring judge, whose only interest in other people, other countries was to study how they'd judge people. When I went to England, I studied their legal system. Studied case law, went to the Inns of Court, to the Old Bailey. I did go once to the theatre, but only to see the Merchant of Venice. I disliked Shakespeare's version of justice. Mischa's wife Helena had on occasions called me an old loner. But I was content. I actually loved my life. That is, until now.

'No, I never got bored with myself,' I said.

'Others probably did,' she said with an impish smile. She was probably right.

'But I am starting to realise,' I tried to explain, 'that there's more to the world than law, courts and lawyers. That people can be viewed in different classifications than just innocent and guilty.'

'That's a funny way of looking at people. Innocent and Guilty. I've never thought of that, even though I love categorising people.'

'Lawyers often do that.'

'Well, so do I: Beautiful and ugly. Musical – non-musical. Hunters – collectors. I'm definitely a hunter. And I don't collect anything. When I want to have something, I work to get it, but once I have it, I immediately lose interest. You?'

'Hmm. I do collect some things. Old legal books. And watches.'

'Watches. That's exactly what I mean. I always wanted a Rolex watch. You know, the commie kids' dream. And with the dosh I made from my first concert I just bought one. And now I'm wearing some second-hand Soviet Army shit again.' She showed me her slender wrist, bearing an oversized green Russian watch with a massive red star on the dial. 'A Rolex is like for special occasions, maybe they'll sponsor me one day.' She bent over to look at my wrist. 'Oh, how predictable. But yours is sort of cool. An old GMT Master, isn't it?' Without waiting for my answer she walked off to get more chai. I watched her walk, her lanky figure. I tried to think what was happening to myself but couldn't understand the answer. How stupid I was, depicting myself as the one-dimensional loner. But then, again, that's the truth. I was. I realised I was such an idiot but could not help it.

'You did a lot of ballet when you were young, didn't you?' I said when she returned.

'How do you know?'

'The way you walk.'

'Yeah. And from the way you talk,' she said, 'you learned Russian in a camp in fucking Siberia.'

'How on earth do you know?'

'You don't talk like a normal Russian.'

'What do you mean?'

'I mean, your language is like they talk in Gulag films.'

'Yes. I actually did learn Russian in Siberia.' I paused, slowly sipping the tea.

'And you speak English and German?'

'No, not really. Only English,' she added. 'We all got trained to speak other languages to spy on you guys. And I had an American boyfriend who spoke no Russian.'

Later we got up and walked slowly back towards the station and took the Metro into town together. When we said goodbye at the stop where I needed to get out, Xenia gave me a hug on the platform and quickly jumped back into the train before the doors could close. Again, I was left alone on the platform, seeing the train disappear into the tunnel. I tried to analyse my feelings but could not come to any wiser conclusion and decided to suppress my emotions again with cognac back at the hotel.

The third time we met, we were wandering aimlessly around Moscow, looking at empty shop windows. I asked Xenia about her studies but she did not want to talk about herself. I somehow felt that she did not want me to ask too many questions. But when she asked me questions, she was very direct. I was not sure how I should react. We kept on walking till Xenia had to dash off to the Conservatory. As I watched her enter the Metro station, I was wondering whether I had botched things up by being so withdrawn, but two days later which I spent in my room, writing away on my legal essay, I found a note from her at the hotel asking me to meet her at the Tretyakov Gallery.

I left the hotel and felt as if I was walking by remote control. One side of me didn't want to go and the other just went ahead. Xenia was waiting for me at the entrance and kissed me on the cheek, smiling warmly. We entered the first room and looked at the paintings. I did not know the artist and thought the style rather dreary. Soon I realised that Xenia was not really interested in the art either and only walked with me to be my tourist guide.

'Is it your first time here?'

'No, I've been before. Seen most of it.'

Suddenly she turned to me.

'Look Max. These paintings are boring. Let's eat ice cream in the sunshine. Tell me about yourself.'

I was slightly taken aback. But she glanced at me with her warm green eyes. I hesitated and realised that I was surprised about myself as I heard myself say to her, 'Do you want to hear the whole story?' She nodded.

We walked out of the gallery into the sunshine.

'I mean, it's pretty long. This might take us till midnight.'

She paused, looking into the distance and then turned to look into my eyes. 'I actually do want to hear it all. Now. It can't be that long, I mean, you are only 65. Look, let's take the Metro and sit in the grass and you tell me. And I promise not to make snide remarks.'

We walked in silence to the Metro station. The train was packed and I was happy to have some time to think. What was I going to tell her? What was I getting into, telling a twenty-five-year-old all about my life? I was crazy. I was trying to imagine what Mischa would say, or his wife. They'd think I'd gone completely mad, hanging out with a girl who could be my grand-daughter. Daughter would be bad enough, but grand-daughter? What was my problem? What was hers? Why was she hanging out with me? All of a sudden, these principal questions came to my head, questions I should have thought about and answered during the last two days. Was her childhood so mucked up that she needed a grand-father figure rather than a father figure or a boyfriend? The Metro stopped and the doors opened. I felt tempted to step out, back into anonymity, away from what would be awaiting me if I opened up to her. The doors remained open even when no one seemed to be left on the platform, but I was glued to my spot and I felt Xenia standing behind me. "Jump. Go. Just bloody leave right now," I heard a voice shouting inside my brain. But my feet were not obeying.

The doors closed. I wiped sweat off my forehead and noticed that my shirt was sticking to my back.

We arrived and got out and were greeted by bright sunshine on the street. In the park we found an empty spot and sat down. Xenia looked at me expectantly.

'Well, let me start from the beginning.'

'Hang on. Let me get some tea. Back in a sec.' She jumped up and soon returned with two glasses of tea.

'Well as a kid I lived in Leipzig where my father taught history at a high school and my mother worked at the local library.' I looked at Xenia, who was lying on my coat in the grass, eyes closed.

'I think I had a pretty protected childhood,' I continued, glancing over at her face to gauge her reactions. But she remained lying on the grass with eyes closed, listening intently. Whenever I stopped, she opened her eyes and looked at me as if to urge me to continue. I opened up to her as I had not opened up to anyone since Julia. I felt vulnerable, but continued, not comprehending why.

My childhood, my little sister Lisa and the role music played in our family. Xenia punched me in the ribs when I said that I didn't care much about music and considered listening to concerts a complete waste of time.

'Hmmm, not sure whether I approve.'

But it was true. My parents had forced me to learn to play the violin but gave up their attempts when I turned 12 and refused to play another note. With hindsight I think they were quite relieved as nothing I ever tried to play sounded better than our neighbour's cats fighting. And at school I was pretty mediocre. And I wasn't particularly good at sports either, or at fighting, and for some reason my classmates appointed me always as their referee. Thinking about it, it was weird that my friends always turned to me when they had an issue where they needed a judge to resolve matters. I judged for everyone. Not only in our class, but also issues older kids got involved in. But if I think about it, at home, I led my life in my private laboratory, completely withdrawn, shielded from what was happening around us.

'But weren't you interested in what's happening around you?'

'Of course I was. I mean, I saw things from my window, in the street, discussed things with my parents who were disgusted by the Nazis. Both thought we were one step away from the abyss.'

'Germany was the fucking abyss,' Xenia said.

I had been asking myself so many times: why did people not wake up? Or were they awake and fully supported what was happening? After the war people claimed that they did not know. But how can you say that when you witnessed Kristallnacht? Only people living in villages can probably make such a claim, but even they could find out if they wanted to. At least I remember it as if it happened yesterday. In the house across the street there was a bookshop. To me it was just a normal bookshop, where you could buy any normal book. From Goethe, Schiller to Hölderlin, Pushkin and Tolstoy, atlases, schoolbooks, maps, some foreign language books. But then during Kristallnacht it became clear what it meant to be a Jewish owner of a 'normal' bookshop. Piles of books were on the pavement and someone poured petrol over them and set them alight. The mob was shouting and, not satisfied with this destruction, completely ransacked the shop.

That day I realised what the Nazis were all about. And later, after the war, when people were saying they did not know how bad the Nazis had been, or that they didn't see things coming, I always had to think about that night and what total idiots and liars people were who were claiming they didn't know. It made me angry every time. I had to think about my sister, who, three years younger than me, realised what was happening. Lisa, who was so fragile and who loved books, music, flowers and animals, who would sit reading all day long and tending to her flowers on our balcony and in the yard behind our house, where she managed to grow all sorts of beautiful plants despite the lack of sunshine. I came to realise how deeply I loved her when the thought of her gave me hope when I was in the prisoner of war camp in Russia all those years, where I felt helpless as I could not be there for her, to protect her. I had always felt the need to protect her as she was very fragile due to months of illnesses when she was young.

'In 1939 the war broke out,' I continued my story.

'No, Max,' Xenia said sitting up. 'That's what all those screwed-up arseholes say today: the war broke out. Like an animal breaking out of the zoo. The war did not break out. The war was fucking deliberately started by fucking Nazi Germany.'

I looked at her, surprised about the outburst.

'It gets into your fucking subconsciousness and then people start believing this shit.'

How can a twenty-something year old have such determined views? But then I guess that Soviet school education was very analytical and dealt with the great war at great length. And then her personal history, her Grandmother's story. Did I have such views when I was her age? Probably, as I had by then been two years at war and some years in camp where thinking or not thinking were the only options and only thinking kept you alive.

'My father had long predicted that Hitler would start another war. More vicious than World War One. And most of my parents' friends thought the same.'

'Did your dad get drafted?'

'Yes. On day one, and only a few weeks later he got killed in Poland.'

'I'm sorry, Max,' Xenia said. 'Awful.'

I remember the evening when we received the news of his death. We were all sitting around the table, too shocked to say anything, just crying. It meant that I became an adult much earlier than I had wanted to. The time for games and building toys was over. School, taking care of Lisa, and doing the household chores my father used to do.

We did not have enough coal to heat the apartment in the winter. We did not have enough food. My mother was broken and spent hours alone in her room each evening when she came back from the library. I had to learn to cook and to steal coal. On top of that, both Lisa and I tried to study English so that we could listen to the BBC and find out what was really happening in the world.

When I turned 18, I got drafted. I had hoped that the war would be over by 1943 despite Hitler, Goebbels and the others on the radio proclaiming we were winning the war on all the fronts.

'By the way, Max. Did you know then what was happening to the Jews? I mean, you experienced Kristallnacht and stuff, but did you really figure out where they all ended up?'

I had to think, not because I did not know the answer, but because the answer was not black and white.

'Yes and no,' I said tentatively. 'I don't think that many people knew about the Final Solution. No-one spoke about the Jews, the Gypsies, about concentration camps. Everyone knew that people were disappearing, never again to be heard of. But no-one seemed to be asking where they were disappearing to. No-one dared to ask the question, I should rather say, as those people who dared to ask questions, disappeared themselves. My mother knew and she told us of camps where they were allegedly held. But she made us swear to keep our mouths shut. She was very scared of losing her job, of the Gestapo, of all the informants who were living amongst us and the slightest critical remark or even question would get you into trouble. The Gestapo were everywhere and their 'Spitzel', informants were omnipresent, also at her library. I don't think, however, that she knew about the gassing that was happening in those camps and if she knew, she tried to protect us from that horrific reality by keeping her knowledge to herself.'

I had to close my eyes as memories flashed up again. Xenia sat up and moved closer and put her arm around me and her head on to my shoulder. I did not know what to do, but then again it seemed to be just natural to her. I was hoping that Xenia was just her usual self, open, friendly, affectionate, like she seemed to be with everyone. We sat in silence, each of us deep in thought. It was getting cooler with the setting sun.

'It's sort of strange. Last time you were here everyone was shooting at you – and you were shooting at them,' Xenia said.

'Well, not quite. I mean, I had five years of peace as prisoner of war.'

'Max, your first bit of sarcasm, you're learning fast,' she laughed.

I looked at the sky where clouds were slowly forming only to be dissolved again by the wind.

'Shall we move? It's getting chilly,' Xenia broke our silence.

'What would you like to do?'

'I'm actually quite hungry. Let's have something to eat? I could cook you something at home and we could wait till Babka comes back. Or go to a restaurant.'

'What would you rather do?'

'Hmm. Not sure. Maybe go to a restaurant. I hardly ever eat out nowadays,' she said. We took the Metro back into town and picked up the car. There was a small cosy place next to her Conservatory, Café Scriabin. When we entered, they welcomed her. Everyone knew her. We sat down and I looked around at the white-washed walls with black and white photos of musicians. I observed the other diners who seemed to be a mix of students and intellectuals. Xenia studied the handwritten menu on the wall and ordered the food and some Georgian wine.

'You didn't finish your story,' Xenia said when our starters were served. 'I mean, what happened in the war. What afterwards.'

'What about yourself?'

'Oh come on. My story isn't half as interesting. Besides, it's pretty short.' She paused, looking at her food, waiting for me to speak.

'If it is so short, why don't you tell me before the main-course arrives,' I said.

'Your sarcasm is getting better, Max,' she said. 'Well, you know some of it. I think that Babka told you about Mum. She was so screwed up. And I don't really know who my father is, though I suspect he's a guy called Victor, a painter. Hmm. I tried to get him to admit it one day when I filled him up with Vodka to make him speak.' She laughed, taking a sip from her glass of wine, 'but he wouldn't budge.' She took another sip. 'This is great wine,' she said.

'Well,' she continued, 'I grew up with Babka. She took care of me. I never saw much of Mum as she was so "busy", well that's what Babka said. She just bloody disappeared for weeks. So I think that when she died, I was shocked and sad, but not really that much. You know? Had Babka died, it would have been the end for me. I mean she brought me up, we had breakfast together, dinner. When there was trouble at school, it was Babka who talked to the teachers, not Mum. In fact, I saw Mum only sometimes at weekends. So, not sure you understand, but in a way, I never had a real mother. The concept of "mother" never existed. For me it was Babka.'

She looked at me, trying to see whether I was listening and then continued.

'Much, much later I started asking the real questions. Who was this woman? Whether I'm like her. I mean, equally mind-fucked.' Xenia paused again and looked at me and then continued. 'Babka explained stuff and I took it all in. I just couldn't cry. So Babka thought I was "internalising my grief" as they called it. And she took me to see a fucking psychologist. But that was such bullshit. I saw her twice and then told her to piss off. That idiot told Babka I'm grieving, suggesting I'm disturbed or vulnerable. I told her she's talking crap, but she just wasn't listening. These psychologists all have their fucking prefabricated boxes. And if you don't fit in, they squeeze you in.'

She laughed.

I looked at her, trying to see whether her laugh was genuine or forced. I could not imagine her not being vulnerable. I mean, as a judge I had seen many kids, teenagers, young people who had come from similarly disturbing backgrounds. Most of them were vulnerable, many turned to drugs, crime, prostitution. But some, very few, were indeed different – if they had grit and talent. Xenia probably had talent and I could sense her determination.

'When I was a teenager,' she continued, 'Victor turned up again one day and left us three paintings, which are worth quite a lot by now as he's gotten famous. Actually, Babka sold two to pay for my tuition. And he taught me to paint when I was sixteen. But he never spoke about Mum or stuff.'

'And what happened to him?'

'Don't know. He comes and goes, sort of drifting in and out. You know, I do like him, even though he's kind of weird.'

She paused to think for a while and then changed the topic abruptly.

'I was OK at school and we had that bloody piano. From the age of three I played every day basically as there was not much else to do. I could have gone outside to play, but in the winter it's too cold and in the summer I got bored. So I just played for hours, teaching myself, but then Babka got me a piano teacher and I started getting serious. And then when Mum died, I just buried myself. Playing for days, basically non-stop. Bloody Chopin Mazurkas and stuff. I guess that's how I got to grips with things, grieving. And I got really good. Then came school, and when I was thirteen, boys, fags, the usual teenage crap. Sex in the school gym after school.'

'You started early.'

'Yeah. Terrible sex though when you're 13. No, wait, terrible sex when the boys are 13. Ha-ha. I also fucked the gym teacher, when I was 15. Babka never found out about all of this.' Again she laughed and then became pensive. 'In a way, it was funny, I felt responsible for her, not the other way around. Of course, she took care of me, but for me it was like I was taking care of her. I came home every night so that she would have someone to talk to. No boys after 7pm was my rule. When she was crying, I comforted her.'

'And when you were crying?'

'Hmm. Don't know. When I was six, I was crying. But then I got over it and decided to toughen up and never cry in front of her. And now I'm OK. I can take punches, but I also have no problem crying in front of you in a restaurant.' She stopped, looking around, but then continued.

'One thing I've learned from all this is that if I ever have children, I'll be very different and very affectionate. I want my kids to know their Mum, love their Mum, even fight with their Mum and still feel her love.'

She stopped and looked at me and caressed my hand. I looked at her hand, her long delicate fingers and chewed-off fingernails.

'Don't look at my hands, Max, they are ugly. I know I shouldn't chew my nails. I can still hear that psychologist say to Babka "chewing nails is a sign of mental instability." I should have punched her.'

'I'd never say that. That's rubbish. I was just observing how long your fingers are,' I lied and had to think for a while about her statement.

I looked at her. Was she really as tough as she tried to appear to be or was there a layer of varnish underneath which lurked a hidden instability? In my work as a judge I had often come across such cases. Kids that looked tough, that had acted tough – that's why they were sitting in front of me, but there were always signs giving away their ultimate vulnerability: chewed finger nails, no eye contact, other signs expressed in non-verbal communication. Except for the finger nails, Xenia did not seem to be that type.

'Goes with the job,' she said, oblivious of my thoughts. 'You need to be able to play an octave. In fact, the moment I was able to play an octave with one hand, I decided to become a pianist.'

'A bit of a weird way to decide?'

'Well, yes and no. From age thirteen I had two things in life: piano and boys. When I started at the Conservatory, I had many boyfriends, fellow-students, artists, actors and two professors. It was great till I was nineteen and then I stopped abruptly. I mean sleeping around. I stopped because I decided to get real bloody serious in life. One hundred per cent piano.'

Xenia looked across the room.

'One day I heard Radu Lupu play Schumann's piano concerto. It was such a fantastic interpretation, so different, that I decided that's it. I wanted to be like him. I spoke to him after the concert and met him again the next day and he asked me to play for him. Such a genius. And I guess that was the end for the boys.'

'So you slept with him?'

'Max, you are horrible. Of course not.'

She paused, thinking, playing with her fork.

'Music is tough. Just bloody practicing for hours on end. No play, no booze, no fags. So, that's where I am.'

She looked at her watch. It was past eleven o'clock.

'We better get going,' I said, looking at her. 'It's late.'

'It's OK. I'm often late.'

When we got up, she looked at me.

'You are such a bloody old misanthrope.' She paused and then added, matter-of-factish, 'and thank you. That was a delicious dinner. And thanks for telling me your story and for listening to mine.' She paused and then said with a quiet voice: 'You probably can't imagine. But this means a lot to me. I normally don't tell people about me.'

Xenia hugged me, when we said goodbye, and I drove back to the hotel. I had left her at her doorstep. That night I could not sleep. Her face, her touch came back into my mind. Was I getting too emotionally entangled? Was she? She seemed to be, but why? Was I the father or grandfather she had been searching for in her life? Or, was she the daughter I'd never had? I struggled as I wanted to free myself and at the same time enter deeper into this unknown world, which showed me sides of myself I hardly knew. But then again when I looked objectively at the situation like a judge would look at a case, I found myself guilty of exploitation of someone who on the surface did not seem weaker, but, adding up all the facts, simply had to fall under the definition of vulnerable. And I, the older person, was taking advantage of my position. But I could not help it.

The next day, I spent sauntering around town, going to the German book shop where I found myself buying the complete works of Goethe for next to nothing. In the early evening I went to the Tretyakov Gallery again but could not concentrate on the paintings as her face and her dark green eyes kept coming up, like in a dream. I looked at the religious paintings, the images of Jesus. Some people would ask God for help to find an answer, but why would God give a damn.

One voice inside me kept on telling me to leave Moscow fast before things got too complicated. And to get back into my shell. The other voice told me to stop listening to the first voice as the first voice had dominated my life all along and got me to where I was now.

I came to think that I had been a man of reason all my life. Judging was an act of reason. Not of emotion, even though my emotional experiences sometimes played a role in my judgments. But most of my emotional experiences date back to the war and to what I witnessed during those years. And to Julia. But I could not deny the validity of the voice of reason. That was me. One hundred per cent.

Fuck. I needed to follow reason, I concluded.

When I passed an Aeroflot office I went in and bought an open business class ticket, one way to Frankfurt. The sales person tried to convince me to reserve a seat on a flight on one of the next days, all flights still had empty seats, but I could not. I felt relieved when I left the office as now, I had the secure knowledge of being able to get out if I decided to. I just needed to pack up my stuff and go to the airport and leave.

Not even that.

I could simply go to the airport and ask the hotel to empty everything from my room and give it to charity. A taxi pulled up on the kerb and I got in.

'Let's go,' I said. The driver looked at me puzzled. 'Just go.'

He drove off, crossing the Moskva river and past the Kremlin and then the Bolshoi theatre where he decided to turn left. We drove on for a while as I glanced out of the window trying to think.

'Sokolniki Park,' I said.

When we reached the park, I asked him to wait. I entered and walked past playing children and grandparents looking after their grandchildren. This could be me. What should I be doing? Be rational, said the rational voice. And I decided to follow it, as I had always done in my life. Successfully.

Getting back into the taxi, the driver stared at me.

'Sheremetyevo.'

'Airport?'

'Yes.'

He drove off, turning onto the pot-hole littered highway. Again he looked at me through the rear-view mirror.

'Are you OK?'

'Sure. Why?'

'You look very troubled. Did your dog die or your wife betray you?' He was great, I had to laugh.

'No, no, I really am OK, and I'm not married.'

'Ah, then you were dumped by your girlfriend.'

I thought why he can't just shut up but his smile was

too sweet to shout at him. We reached the airport at last and I got out and paid him.

'Shall I wait for you?'

'No, I'm flying out, don't worry.'

'Hmm. You don't look like it. No luggage. Not even a briefcase like a banker or a lawyer.'

I tipped him and went into the terminal. The business class queue was short. I handed the check-in lady my ticket. She looked at it.

'Anything to check in, Dr Hardenberg?'

'Nothing.'

'Window or aisle?'

'Window.'

'3A?'

I nodded and took the boarding card and headed for security. I had not called the hotel.

In the lounge I gulped down a large glass of whisky. Chivas. The taste took a weight off my shoulders. I would be home. Finally home, normality. I filled myself another glass and a third. I was thinking straight again, but yet I could still hear the voice inside me urging me to stop being an idiot and face reality, to listen to my feelings and to stop suppressing feelings and emotions. I didn't really want to recognise this voice but the more I listened to it the more I felt the urge to hear more. Over the loudspeaker I heard a voice calling a Dr Hardenberg to go to the gate as the plane was ready to depart. I ignored the voice and poured the rest of the bottle into my glass. The voice called my name again. My internal voice turned annoyingly rational, arguing not to let this once in a lifetime opportunity pass. The opportunity to change, to leave one-dimensionality behind, to open up and fully live. Was this now the rational voice? I sat down and looked at the screen. Flights were boarding for London and my flight showed up as closed. Then it dropped off the screen. I remained sitting in the lounge till it too closed.

I went back to the hotel and went to bed. What an idiot I was. Although I had taken a decision, I tried to persuade myself that I had not taken a decision. It was only in the morning that I saw the note stuck under my door.

'Please come and visit me at the Conservatory.
Love X'

I had a pretty bad hangover but the former rational voice was gone. At ten o'clock I was walking down the corridors, trying to find the room where she might be. I should have looked at the back of her note. Room 443. I rushed up the stairs and stopped in front of the door. Silence. I knocked and, as no-one answered, entered. The room was empty. I looked around. A grand piano was standing at the other end of the room, there were a couple of chairs and a green armchair near the window. I decided to sit down in the armchair and wait. From the neighbouring room, I heard voices, a male voice and Xenia's voice, arguing.

'You're nuts,' the man shouted. 'You're wasting your life.'

Then there was silence. I could not hear what the woman was answering till she raised her voice.

'... and so what, Boris. I honestly don't give a fuck. Plus it's none of your fucking business.'

I decided to leave as I didn't want to spy on their conversation, but I heard the door shutting with a bang. I thought Xenia would enter straight away and got up, but I heard her footsteps walking away down the corridor. I sat down again, thinking what the conversation might have been about. I closed my eyes and other thoughts entered my head: our walk on the Lenin Hills, her hug. I felt warmth and tingling in my stomach and the sunshine on my face and the breeze in the air, birds singing. I looked around and there were deep forests and the lake in which Mischa and I had been swimming. I remember that I was thinking, how can that be, as I was supposed to be in Moscow, but Natasha was leaning against a nearby tree and told me not to worry, that Xenia was coming by soon. A German Jeep appeared with two soldiers, and for some reason, Olaf was in the Jeep. I wanted to get up, but couldn't, which was strange.

I awoke when her hands touched my shoulders. I had not heard her enter the room. 'You were deep asleep, Max. Thank God, you weren't snoring.' She laughed and embraced me as I got up.

'I'm so glad you came. I feared you might have buggered off to Munich as there was radio silence.' She looked at me with a serious face and finally turned to the piano. 'Hey, let me play something for you.'

She swiftly sat down and started playing. First, she was looking at me to gauge my reaction but then she closed her eyes as if to dive deeper into the music. She only opened them again when she had played the last note and got up. 'Do you like it? Guess who's the composer?'

Thank God I knew this piece, as you had to listen to it when my secretary's phone was occupied.

'Chopin. Some Mazurka, I believe.'

'Damn. Spot on. C sharp minor. You're really good. And I thought you knew nothing about music. Let me play you some more. I really love his music.'

I sat back and listened to her playing. She held her eyes closed and gently swayed back and forward as she was playing. When she had finished, she looked up.

'What next?'

'Rachmaninoff, please.'

'OK. Let me see.'

Again, she closed her eyes and played, fast, furiously hammering the notes. One could feel that Rachmaninoff was her music. She loved the sound she could get out of the piano, playing fortissimo as if in fury. Exhausted she stopped and I walked over to her, standing behind her seat, putting my hands on to her shoulders. She touched and held them. 'Let me play you some more. But stay like that, please.'

She started playing the first movement of Beethoven's Moonlight sonata, with immense feeling, a very unusual interpretation, even I could hear that.

'Beautiful. I really loved it,' I said when she had

stopped. 'You know, Rachmaninoff was great, because it was so powerful. I loved the way you played it. But this piece was maybe even more beautiful in its own way.'

'What do you mean?'

'In the way, you put your feelings into it,' I tried to explain. She pulled me towards her and embraced me gently.

We had lunch at Café Scriabin but did not stay long and went back together to the hotel.

'I'm so tired.' She yawned and lay down on the bed, stretching her arms. 'Come, join me.' I sat down beside her, caressing her hair. She closed her eyes. After a few minutes she had fallen asleep. I got up and started reading one of the books I had bought, poems by Goethe. Soon, also I felt drowsy but decided to sleep in the armchair rather than joining Xenia in bed, which I felt was not right. It was dark, when we both woke up. She was sitting on the chair beside me, looking at me through the darkness, caressing my hand.

'I feel so happy when I'm with you, Max. And safe. The world could stop spinning and I couldn't give a damn when I'm with you.' She paused and got up. 'But I need to go.'

'Let me drive you home,' I said.

'No way. I'm OK taking the Metro,' she said, kissing me goodbye.

It was late in the morning when I called Mischa. I had given him the telephone number of the hotel and had asked him to call me as soon as he'd received the results of the tests. I was getting nervous about his silence. But when I got him on the phone, he sounded chirpy. No, nothing new, he was feeling great, chopping wood and working in the garden.

I did not tell him about Xenia but promised that I'd call again in a few days. I felt relieved that he was fine. But then, again, I thought he was sounding just a bit too cheerful. Was this real?

Xenia and I met up later in the day. We had a late lunch, again at Scriabin, but she had no time to walk about, so I sat and listened to her practicing certain passages of a Rachmaninoff piece again and again. Practicing is hard work, repetitive and demanding. I tried to hear the differences but failed to understand what sounded wrong or why something sounded better.

The next evening when we returned to the hotel, Xenia quickly undressed and went straight to bed. I was not sure what to do and, when I was not sure, I turned to Cognac. Eventually, I lay down beside her, on the duvet, fully dressed. She put her head on to my shoulder and fell asleep. Still, nothing happened. As she had said, I realised that maybe she was just not at all interested in sex. And I was definitely too shy or too self-conscious to make the first move.

Every day she seemed to be coming a bit closer in her embraces, and when she kissed my cheeks, her lips were touching mine. And when we talked, she was asking many questions about the past, about my time as a prisoner of war, and life at the Eastern front. It was strange as on the one hand, I experienced her as a young and carefree student, with wild ideas. And on the other hand, she was mature, thoughtful, with an understanding for things, feelings, doubts, that few fifty-year-old adults have. She was almost like a psychoanalyst, digging deeper into the layers of my past. And the deeper she dug and the more affectionate she became the more I realised the ground underneath me was giving in, as if it was ice melting over the warm waters of a suddenly erupting geyser. My mind was taken and I was only thinking about her, wanting to be with her. I did not understand myself anymore as she gently pulled me out of my one-dimensionality and reclusiveness. Sheremetyevo airport seemed a long time ago.

We returned from our walk on the Red Square and I lay down on the bed and continued reading. I had started *Faust*, the first part and was immediately drawn into the medieval world, travelling with Faust and Mephistopheles, when she nestled up to me and started unbuttoning my shirt without saying anything. I hesitated. I had been thinking about kissing her – but we had not even kissed. Was I a dirty old man, exploiting a young vulnerable kid? Or was I being exploited by someone who had told me herself that she'd slept around a lot. When did I last sleep around? I could just as well have been working as a Catholic priest for the last years that I lived in celibacy (and sleeping with the occasional colleague's colleague as Catholic priests presumably do). Did Gretchen seduce Faust?

I turned to her and looked into her eyes, but in the end

only managed to stammer: 'Xenia, I... I don't think it's right.'

She looked at me not comprehending. 'At least not yet,' I added quickly. She turned around, facing the pillow. Faust was so much more convincing.

'And when would it be right?' she paused. 'Is there a time when making love is wrong or right? I don't get it. Why are you always so distant? You're pushing me away when I hug you and turn your face when I try to kiss you on your mouth. Max. What is it?'

'But do you realise, how old I am?'

'Look, Max, I really don't give a shit.'

'I just feel it has to wait.'

'Wait? What for? Till you are 85? You'll be bloody impotent by then. Next week all this may be over and you'll be gone, back to Germany, and when will I see you again?'

'Please, Xenia.'

'Please? What do you mean, please?' She became silent and then turned around to look at me.

'Maybe you don't realise. But I can't stand the thought of you leaving just the way you arrived. You came by one day, caused total fucking chaos in my life, can't you see? And now you simply want to say goodbye, pack your bloody Jeep and drive back to Germany, never to be seen again? What the fuck. No.' I saw how she was fighting tears. She wiped her eyes.

'I won't let you go just like that,' she continued. 'I don't know why, but you mean far too much to me, Max. You mean much more to me than any of the bloody boys I've been fooling around with. They were fuck-wit kids, Max. With you it's different.'

'But Xenia, I'm too old. You need someone with a future.'

'Max. Please. I've had an affair with a seventy-five-year-old conductor. I'm not that impressed by your age. Sorry to be so blunt. I don't feel the difference between you and me and I don't want to be going out with boys of my age. Besides, I'll be fifty-five when you'll die aged ninety-five. I'll find someone of my age then, when they've grown up.' She paused and lay back, looking at the ceiling.

'If I really gave a damn, do you think I'd be here with you? I mean, can't you see?' She turned on her back and remained silent. I did not know what to say until she whispered, 'Please Max. Don't just leave me again.'

I caressed her hair, her face, feeling her soft skin.

'No Xenia. Don't worry. I won't disappear just like that, I promise. And certainly not tomorrow – you mean far too much to me too. It's strange, but I cannot imagine a day without seeing you.' We lay in silence, as I took her into my arms, caressing her. But Xenia was restless and eventually got up. 'I'm going home, Babka needs me. She's been very strange lately, very upset and I don't know why.'

We left the hotel together and I continued to walk around when Xenia had gone. It was just after midnight, but the air felt warm and pleasant. I sat down on a bench and wanted to smoke a cigar to think about our relationship, but instead, thoughts of Karl Heinz Hempe came drifting into my head, even though I did not want to think about him anymore. I bought a cigar from a late-night seller who walked the streets with his tray full of candy and cigarette packets in front of him and sat down on the bench again. I wanted to buy a Bolivar but he only sold Romeo y Julieta. I had to smile when I lit it and watched the smoke rise in the darkness. How appropriate. Smoking always helped to think and deal with things. The taste was sad and bitter, like my memories.

Hempe

At school Hempe was the first one who had joined the Hitler Youth, when all of us were still playing Cowboys and Indians, and none of us had the faintest interest in finding out what the Nazis were all about. But Hempe was different. He was a young fascist. Already back in 1937 he terrorised the school with his Hitler Youth friends, all of whom were little bullies.

Mosche Schlemmer, our physics teacher came to my mind. He was lucky as he got beaten up by Hempe and his gang and, as a result, shortly afterwards emigrated to the US. I should have written to him after the war but could not get myself to do it, even when I read an article about him in the papers. By then he had become a professor at Princeton.

I despised Hempe who was a bully when he was with his friends but a complete coward when he was alone. Like most bullies he needed his group for support. We once had a fight. He had made advances to my sister, Lisa, and could not take 'no' for an answer and continued molesting her, groping her in front of his friends. Lisa cried, and tried to get away. She was nine or ten. His friends just laughed and no one interfered. The next day at school I got him alone in the corridor and warned him never to touch my sister again. His face turned white and I aimed for his solar plexus and punched as hard as I could. Pure pain. My second punch landed straight in his face. The coward did not fight back, instead he winced, begging me to let him go. I turned and left him kneeling on the floor. I was naïve and should have expected revenge. The same afternoon, Hempe cornered me with five of his friends. None of them would have taken me on alone. They dragged me into the toilet and beat me up, kicking me in the face, in the stomach, jumping on my back. I smelled urine as I was lying on the floor, unable to get up. Then they were gone. I crawled to the loo and pulled myself up, sitting down, crying because of pain and anger. My lips were swollen, I touched them with my tongue. They tasted of urine and the bitterness of bile. My eyebrows were bleeding as the skin had burst open. Outside, miraculously, was Julia. She helped me clean my face and my wounds and took me to see Dr Rosenstein who stitched me up. When I left the surgery, she was crying. I was too bitter and angry to cry, even though all my bones and my stomach were hurting. She took my hand and we walked home together.

I relit my cigar which had gone cold as I was following my thoughts. Even in the darkness the rising smoke seemed blue, not grey. I felt some distant anger thinking back that Hempe never got punished. But then again, I felt some satisfaction that soon afterwards he left school as he wasn't bright enough to pass the Abitur, our finals. And during the war I forgot all about him. The front was full of Hempes.

And then I encountered them again, when I was finally freed. Finally, I thought to myself, I should be happy. Finally free after five years in camp. Soon I would have peace, food, no cold, no more hunger. It was unbelievable to be walking through the gates of the camp, the train journey that seemed never ending, then more familiar fields, houses, villages, and around four am in the morning Leipzig station. I got off, not recognising much.

I was walking down the street, our street. I looked around thinking that calling this street my street felt wrong. The cobble stones were still the same. Some were damaged, probably from tanks or shrapnel. But mostly they seemed the same. I remembered walking here barefoot years ago. How fast everything had changed. Barefoot in 1935, playing football as a ten-year-old. But now? Everything that used to make it our street seemed gone, the houses had been bombed, the trees chopped, the shops destroyed. Instead of houses, there were some walls that had been left standing and then vast areas of barren land. What was I looking for?

The house with the bookshop had been flattened completely so that one could see straight through into the distance. Our house was gone too, destroyed by a direct hit. I thought of my mother, sensing her presence in the earth that was there beneath the rubble. Why had they not rebuilt our house or the bookshop? I looked around dumbfounded but then slowly started to realise that for some reason this destruction also filled me with satisfaction instead of the initial sadness and emptiness. It was as if someone had taken revenge on my behalf to obliterate everything that could remind me of the Nazi years before I got drafted.

Heading back to the station, I noticed a man walking purposefully as if he was going to some important meeting. Maybe he was. I looked at him as he came nearer and he looked at me and he slowed down.

'Max?' he said.

Karl Heinz Hempe. The last person I wanted to meet.

Dressed in civilian clothes, he looked quite smart in contrast to my haggard appearance in my dirty and torn clothes that were far too big to fit me as I was not much more than a skeleton after years in camp. Before I could open my mouth, he rushed up to me and said again, 'Max. Amazing. How good to see you.'

Before I could do anything, he gave me a bear-like hug.

'So you've survived,' he grinned and shook my hand.

'I just got back,' I replied.

'Where from?'

'Russia. Camp.'

He looked at me and beamed.

'Thank God it's all over. Also for you. Thank God the horror's ended.'

These words entered my brain, as if in slow motion. Horror he had said, he of all people. I couldn't believe it and remained silent. This was Karl Heinz Hempe at his best. I felt weak and thought I'd tasted bitterness of bile and urine, like back on that day when he had beaten me up. I just stood there, dumbfounded, whilst he continued waffling that it had been a terrible time, but that now it's all over, and, better, there is the new beginning. *Neuanfang* and *Wiederaufbau*, were his words – new beginning and reconstruction. Like millions he was going to forget the past. No. He had already forgotten the past during the last five years and had started a career in the new world.

'Don't think, Karl Heinz, that I can forget things so easily. You were one of them,' I said quietly, looking into his piggish face. 'I bet you didn't even serve in the war.'

'I was needed here in Leipzig,' he replied. 'I helped with the evacuation during the bombing raids. Besides, you're wrong, Max, I wasn't a Nazi. Everyone was wearing brown shirts. I was a *Mitläufer*.'

Mitläufer. Literally, the ones who are running along. Everyone had been only a *Mitläufer* all of a sudden.

I was speechless for a moment, and then just said: 'Don't give me that shit, Hempe.'

He froze and his pig face turned sour. He took a step back and said with a loud voice, 'you'd better be careful. The Allies are still checking on everyone. You were at the front, and the new Germany doesn't need war criminals.'

What an arsehole, I thought, and felt like spitting into his face.

'Just piss off,' I said and turned around and walked away. This wasn't my street anymore. Leipzig not my town. It was time to move on.

Julia

The next day, I wanted to meet Xenia where I had stopped the evening before. We sat down on the same bench and I lit another cigar which I bought from the same guy, walking with the tray around his neck. 'New stock,' he said, smiling. 'The Count.'

I did not understand and smiled back.

'Let me try it,' Xenia said, taking the cigar from me. 'It does not taste bad at all.' She puffed. 'Hmm. I quite like the taste and I thought cigars are only for bloody capitalists.'

'Or communists.'

She looked at the label. 'Right. Monte Cristo. That's the stuff that Chez used to smoke, isn't it?' I had no idea. Chez. The doctor who became an idol for the West's idiotic kids because of his motorbike even though he had gone around shooting people randomly. Suddenly the Havana just didn't taste right.

'Did Julia smoke with you?'

I shook my head.

'How did you guys get back together again after the war?' Xenia suddenly asked.

'I found her through my sister.'

'Were you looking for her or was it a coincidence?'

It was annoying that Xenia always found my weak

points. Julia was the thought that had kept me alive in the trenches and in camp. The thought of her eyes, her smile. I had fallen in love with her after I had been drafted, when I was hiding from flying shrapnel, when I was hungry and freezing in camp. So straight after I got to Munich, I tried to find her, hoping she would have survived and hoping she would fall in love too.

'She moved into my tiny apartment and we had years of happiness, just bliss, fun, life without any clouds on any horizon. She was working as a teacher at the local high school, teaching classics and sport – a weird combination. In the evenings we used to sit together on our balcony, she was correcting exercises or preparing lessons, whilst I was studying. Or we went to the theatre together or met with friends.'

I glanced over to Xenia, who was very different, I thought.

'You know what was strange was that she had absolutely no ear for music and no interest in any form of art, like paintings, sculptures, whatever. We went to the mountains every weekend, going hiking or rock climbing in the summer and skiing in the winter. In 1951 her grandfather had died and she had inherited a house, or, rather, a hut, just outside Alpbach, a village in Austria. Whenever we could, we would go there and spend all our weekends and holidays in our hut.'

'Hmm. So you just made love in your hut all day long?'

'Ha ha, not really. I mean, Julia was quite a contrast to me, very sociable with many friends and always happy.'

'Whereas you are introverted and grumpy,' Xenia said.

'Well, you're laughing. But I think you're right in a way.'

'I guess you get grumpy when your main social interaction is with criminals and lawyers.'

Alpbach

We were climbing up the mountains behind Inner Alpbach. It was warm again, and the sun was burning on the grass that smelled intensely as it was freshly cut. Gradually the path got steeper and I turned around and saw Julia looking at me. I struggled as her face expressed desperation.

'I'm just so exhausted, darling.' She stopped to regain her breath. We had almost reached the Farmkehr Alm and slowly continued till we saw it around the corner.

'Please just go ahead, I will stay here and have a bite to eat.'

I kissed her and left her sitting at the Alm and started climbing alone. I looked at the amazingly blue sky, with no cloud on the horizon and loved speeding through the grass towards the peak, but all of a sudden it struck me and I turned around and ran down the mountain. Julia was sitting in the sunshine.

'You have to see a doctor,' I said.

She just smiled at me.

'I'll be OK, don't worry.'

On Monday afternoon, Julia went to see a doctor in Munich. We waited anxiously the whole week. Friday, she got the results. Cancer. And the tumour had spread all through her body.

Why? I held her in my arms and could not speak. Why? Julia just smiled and remained calm.

'Let's cook some spaghetti,' she said matter of factly and went to the kitchen.

I threw myself on to the floor not wanting to believe what I had heard. I banged my head against the floor boards. Why. But now the why had a different meaning. Why had I been so careless. Why had I not taken her to see a doctor earlier? Why had I, the lawyer with the sharp eye for detail, ignored the now so obvious signs.

Julia could be heard from the kitchen as if nothing else was happening to her.

I cried and she was comforting me, I just could not stop though I was aware that I should be the one supporting her. We ate in silence and went to bed. I wanted to feel her warm body and hold her in my arms, her naked skin. We kissed and made love and lay awake till dawn. In the early morning we drove back to the mountains. On Sunday night, we closed the shutters, feeling this might be the last time in our hut for a long time.

Four months later Julia died and I withdrew.

Hermit

'I'm sorry,' Xenia said. 'That really is horrible, Max.'

Those thoughts still made me sad and those last weeks remained deeply ingrained in my memory, as if they were condensed into a never-changing yesterday. I felt how my throat was tightening. In silence we walked through the lobby and took the lift to our floor.

'After that did you have another girlfriend?'

I hesitated and then said, 'No, to be honest, I didn't. I worked, judged, did some research and in my free time did a PhD and then a post-doc degree. I did not really want to make new friends. Sometimes I went to the movies, and sometimes I went up to Alpbach to our hut, but it had lost its charm for me and so I gave it to her cousin.'

'So, after Julia, that was it, you're saying?' Xenia asked.

'Well, yes and no. I mean, I still had a number of, call it relationships, or short-term affairs, but I never felt like loving someone again. I had a relationship for many years with a legal aid who was working for one of my colleagues, but it was not love, just mutual loneliness, and then, ten years ago it finished as she got married.'

'And you never fell in love again?'

'That's a bit difficult, when you're over fifty,' I said.

'You really are a bit sad, and a bit weird,' Xenia said, caressing my head.

I called room service for a bottle of wine. We drank it silently. I thought, I was drinking far too much wine with Xenia. Did I always drink that much?

'And Hempe?'

I turned around to look into her eyes.

'It was many years later that my sister told me that during the war Hempe had raped Julia. It had happened during an air-raid. They were together in a bunker, alone. She couldn't escape because bombs were falling left right and centre, so he raped her.'

'I'm sorry. Awful.'

Hempe

What's equally awful I thought many times is that he never got punished for it. He never got punished for anything. But he could not fool me, as it was very clear that he was not only riding the wave but that he was actually part of the force that waves need to sustain themselves. He was a bigwig with the Nazis, and she was not. And the police wouldn't do a thing, of course. And once the war was over, people had different things on their minds. As it seemed that almost every woman got raped by Soviet soldiers, rape as such simply got pushed aside, pushed out of one's consciousness as people didn't want to deal with it, as it was too ghastly.

But my sister couldn't forget him. She stayed on in Leipzig, despite the fact that it soon became evident that the new regime in the East was not much better than fascism. Lisa became a teacher hoping to escape the socialist bureaucracy and tyranny by being a good teacher.

'Up to 1961 we managed to see each other every few months and then the East Germans built the wall in Berlin, cutting off the East from the West.'

'I remember. We needed to build the wall to keep out the fascist imperialists,' Xenia said sarcastically.

'Well, in 1970 Lisa bumped into Hempe again. He went after her. Lisa resisted his approaches but he became violent and tried to rape her too. In contrast to Julia, she managed to punch him and escape.'

'That's gutsy,' Xenia said.

'She lost her job as a teacher. Hempe had by now become an East-German party apparatchik and influential in the administration of Leipzig. She had to work in a factory and he remained untouched.'

'Disgusting.'

'At least she managed to continue to run a kids group in the evenings for the workers of the factory.'

I looked at Xenia and we continued walking in silence. We had turned into a small street. The cobble stones were uneven. Xenia stopped and took off her shoes. Slowly, she walked on barefoot, like I used to do as a kid in Leipzig, I thought.

Hempe got promoted to Berlin and went to work for the Ministry of Interior and then for the Ministry of Economics. But for Lisa it was only at the end of the seventies, when she got a new boss, that she no longer had to work at a conveyor belt but could run the factory's kindergarten full time.

'Every year I went to Leipzig to meet with her at the time of the annual trade fair. I pretended to be the boss of a small business producing car rear-view mirrors.'

'That's quite funny,' Xenia observed. 'But why didn't you try to get her out?'

'She wouldn't leave.'

'That's admirable. I doubt they appreciated it.'

Again we walked in silence, turning back on to a busy road. Xenia put on her shoes again. We could see our hotel in the distance.

'Let's not turn back yet, Max. How did Hempe die?'

'It happened about a few months after the wall came down.'

'So you were still working.'

Wannsee

It was a strange day. Finally, the door opened and Lisa entered the Café Savigny where I had been waiting. She was looking for me and for a few seconds, I observed her, how frail she had become. Then she saw me and beamed. We hugged for a long time and sat down to eat. Café Savigny is in the western part of Berlin – she definitely did not want us to meet up in a restaurant in the East.

'Let's have some decent French wine,' she said. 'After years of that Soviet or Bulgarian piss, I deserve some good Bordeaux.' She chose a bottle of Chateau Chasse Spleen.

'This is amazing stuff,' she said when the waiter ceremoniously had poured the wine.

'Do you want to own shares in our company?' she asked and told me about their plans to take over her factory. The management and the workers had got together to buy it in order to avoid it being bought up by foreigners or the ex-Stasi clique. I was not so sure.

Later that evening we took the S-Bahn back to Wannsee, where we were staying in a small hotel at the lake. It was late and we were walking along the shore when we saw a figure approaching. Lisa immediately recognised him. Karl Heinz Hempe. She grasped my arm and I could feel her fear even though there was nothing to fear. Pictures of him as a Hitler Youth flashed into my mind, and of him raping Julia. And when we were about to pass one another, he looked up and recognised us. He stopped, smiling broadly.

'How nice to see you, Lisa. And, can it be true, Max. After so many years,' he said, grabbing our hands, blabbing away.

'Why don't we sit down for a moment or we can meet for lunch tomorrow if you want,' he said.

We sat down on the small wall bordering the lake.

'It's so amazing to see you and to be here in Berlin after all those years of bloody communism.' We could not believe our ears and remained silent.

'Finally a market economy for all of us and freedom of speech, justice.'

We felt like puking.

'And you know what? I've got a buyer for your factory in Leipzig, Lisa, and I will run it. Isn't that wonderful? We have to fire the old boss, he knows nothing. Different times now. Different times.'

I looked into Lisa's eyes and she looked into mine. What Hempe was talking about faded into the background. We looked around, there was no one except us.

'You tried to rape me. Twice!' Lisa hissed. 'And you raped Julia.'

His blabbering stopped.

'No... I... I,' he stammered.

'You're such a liar. Arsehole,' I said.

We both understood immediately. Lisa quickly grabbed his feet and I gave him a push and he disappeared over the wall. It seemed to take a long time till we heard the splash and then there was silence. Hempe had made no efforts to swim.

I looked at Lisa but she just observed the darkness underneath us without saying anything. As the waves subsided, total silence set in.

Lisa sighed, as if freed from some tremendous nightmare.

'That's what justice is about,' she concluded.

We looked down and saw his body drifting away into the black lake.

A few days later we were back in Leipzig and in Munich. The papers reported that his body had been found. The police thought it was an accident and ruled out foul play. I had to smile when Lisa read me the article over the phone.

Breakfast

We had reached the hotel again and walked through the lobby. We took the lift back to our floor and went to our room. When the door had closed behind us, Xenia put her arms around my neck and looked seriously into my eyes.

'So, that was the second person you judged and killed. The first one being my – eh – grandfather.' She paused for a moment. 'Judge Max.'

She walked over to the bottle of wine that was still standing on the table and filled both glasses, taking one and sipping slowly.

'I guess you'll hate me for this,' I said, looking at her.

Xenia walked to the other side of the room and sat down on a chair. She remained silent for a while, just sipping intermittently from her glass. In the end she shook her head.

'No. You did the right thing, Max. I would not have jumped into the lake to rescue Hempe either. What a piece of shit.' She looked at her glass and added after a pause:

'Thou shalt not kill is too holy for this fucked-up world.'

I lay down on the bed and Xenia joined me. We remained silent for a while, listening to the noise on the street in the distance.

'Please don't drive back to Germany soon,' she suddenly said, turning to look at me.

'Don't worry. I don't want to go back, yet. I can't go back now that I am just starting to discover you.' She closed her eyes.

'I promise,' I added after a while, listening to her breathing, that had become slow and regular. I caressed her face but realised she had fallen asleep.

I woke up as the sun was shining into my eyes. Xenia was standing at the window, dressed only in a t-shirt.

'Sweet dreams?'

'Hmm. Don't quite remember,' I said. 'I think I was dreaming we were in Oleg's garden and he was saying something like 'Justice. Light and Justice. Or, the sun brings justice. Weird.'

'Let's go and have breakfast now. I think you need a double espresso to talk about justice.'

I went to the bathroom to take a shower.

'Can't you dream of anything else but justice?' I heard her shout. 'You're seriously weird.'

I felt the water on my head and closed my eyes, standing like that for minutes, enjoying the warmth. Suddenly, I felt her hands on my shoulders. I turned around. She was standing naked, innocent. I looked at her slender body, her light brown skin, her small breasts. She hugged me, pressing her body against mine. I felt the softness of her breasts as her mouth touched mine. We kissed.

Xenia felt light and ethereal as we made love. Time did not exist. We had breakfast around three in the afternoon in our room and continued as if life outside had stopped.

'Today I really need to get up and go to class,' Xenia said the following morning. I looked at the clock. It was just after six am.

We were the only ones at breakfast. We drank espresso and munched on our croissants, still half asleep.

I walked around town whilst she attended her lectures, needing time on my own to think. I was sauntering aimlessly about, trying to find answers to the questions which were repeating themselves in my mind. Maybe I should ask Mischa what he thought about it. But then again, it had happened. We had made love. I was in love.

I picked up Xenia for lunch from the conservatory. We had soup and fresh bread at Scriabin and she had to rush back to practice. In a bookshop I came across a thick book full of black and white photos of people walking the streets of Moscow. The photos were good, some were sharp, others grainier, every shot a piece of art. I decided that at some stage I also wanted to take up photography – something I had never done in my life. I bought the book.

Xenia looked up when I entered the room and allowed me to sit down at the other end, whilst she was playing parts of Rachmaninoff. She played fast and furiously, repeating the same passage time after time after time, taking no notice of her surroundings. Then she played Bach and it was as if her character had changed. She sat still, listening intently to the music she was playing and the music that was playing inside her head, her eyes closed. She played an Adagio, a complete contrast to the brutal fury of Rachmaninoff. Bach sounded abstract to me, like maths. I loved just sitting there, listening to her playing, trying to get to know her better by understanding the way she interpreted the various pieces.

When the Conservatory closed for the day, we went to have dinner at her grandmother's place. She looked at me when she got into the Jeep and said, 'You know, Max. It's always you who's driving. Let me have a go one day.'

'Can you drive?'

'Oh, bugger off. Of course I can. Old Volgas and Ladas.'

'I didn't know you were interested in cars,' I said.

'Well, no, not really. I mean how can you be interested in cars in a country that just produces such crap-mobiles. I think I'd love to drive a real car, like a Jaguar. I once saw one of those sleek two door things, XJS I think it was. That's my kind of car.'

I did not know what to answer, as I had no interest in cars at all.

'You are such a capitalist.'

'I know.'

We drove silently through the traffic, overtaking the many trolleybuses that were making their way to the suburbs, people crammed inside. Whilst I parked the Jeep, Xenia went upstairs. She waved to me from the fifth floor to come up. The door was open when I arrived and Natasha was smiling broadly.

'And I thought you had left us already. It's so nice of you to come by again. Glad you can stay for supper. Sorry, I haven't prepared much,' she said.

'Oh, don't worry, I'm happy with a piece of bread or some potatoes,' I said.

'Look, Babka, we brought you some wine from the hotel,' Xenia said.

We sat down around the table which Natasha had prepared for us. I opened the bottle of wine and as soon as I had poured a glass, Xenia took it and took a long sip. I looked at her as this was normally a sign that something bothered her.

'Well, Moscow has not changed that much since Brezhnev died,' Natasha said.

'I did not really know the city before, but it looks lively and waking up, like out of a slumber.'

'Gorbachev is such a disaster.'

'Come on, Babka, it's thanks to him that you can now read every author you want without resorting to some *Samizdat* edition.'

'True.'

I was again surprised by her knowledge of western authors. She knew Max Frisch better than me and had read most of Solzhenitsyn.

'You know, everything that was hidden is coming out now, and we have a lot of history that was dark, murky if not downright evil, which we have to unveil,' Natasha said.

'Our history is much darker than Stalin's, though,' I said.

'I'm not sure I would agree,' said Natasha pensively. 'Stalin was at least as evil as Hitler but he lacked the organisational discipline to murder on an industrial scale.'

'He was a genocidal fuckwit,' Xenia said.

We continued eating in silence. I loved the dark and somewhat earthy taste of the cabbage, which Natasha had slightly fried with some fine pieces of garlic and onions. The wine was heavy, from the Grusinskaja Republic, grown near the Black Sea. I looked at Xenia and realised that something was still going on in her head. She was eating absent-mindedly, chewing almost mechanically. I let her get on with her thoughts and savoured the food instead.

Suddenly Xenia turned to me with a serious face.

'I've been trying to think about this, Max,' she started. 'I don't really know whether you know, but I feel I have to ask you: Are you sure that my grandmother's rapist was really dead when you shot him?'

I looked at her, surprised, putting my fork down.

'Absolutely. I shot him twice and my friend Mischa checked on him. He was dead. Definitely dead.'

'And the other guy?'

'Please, Xsjusha,' Natasha interjected. 'That's over. Past. I don't care. And if I don't care, you shouldn't care either.'

'No, Babka. I do care. So, Max, what about the other guy. Was he dead too?'

'No. I shot him and hit him but I didn't finish him off,' I said, feeling that pang of guilt, again.

'So he's still walking around, free.'

'Possibly. I don't know,' I said, knowing well that

probably he was alive. 'If he survived my bullets, the war, maybe prisoner of war camp, and another forty-five years then he might still be alive.'

'Do you know who he was? I mean, do you know his name?'

'Yes,' I said

'Hmmm.'

'Please, Xsjusha. Can't you let go?' Natasha said annoyed. 'It really shouldn't bother you. I don't want to think about it. Can't you see it's painful for me to think about this? To bring it up again?'

'But we have to have justice, Babka. We have to deal with the dark patches of our history as a nation, you said it yourself, and we have to deal with our own, personal history too, Babka. We have to.'

'But it hurts. I have worked through my history. And I've moved on. Besides, what justice is it that comes some forty – fifty years later? It hurts me more than him,' Natasha said, pain reflected on her face. 'You can't imagine, how painful it is to think about this again. I can't. You know I can't. You know I cannot even go back to our house. I want to bury everything. Every thought.'

Natasha looked at Xenia and then put her hands in front of her face and started sobbing. Xenia looked down at her plate.

'I'm sorry, Babka. I didn't want to hurt you. Really. I hadn't realised.'

She got up and walked around the table and stood behind her grandmother, putting her arms around her.

'Please, Babka, don't cry.' She whispered into her ear, stroking her hair.

I got up and left the room and went to the landing in front of the apartment door lighting my pipe, pretending to need to smoke. After a while Xenia came out.

'Please come back in, Max,' she said with a sad and quiet voice. 'I honestly hadn't realised.'

When I walked back in, Natasha was sitting at the table, her eyes still red.

'Sorry, Max. I shouldn't have cried like that,' she said.

'No, please, Natasha. I can imagine how you feel. What your memories must be like. Also I sometimes have memories coming up and… it's awful.'

'Thank you,' she said. 'But I guess you don't cry.'

'It may surprise you, but sometimes I do,' I said.

We ate our dessert of fresh strawberries with cream in silence. When we had finished the coffee, I decided to go back to the hotel. Xenia wanted to stay with her grandmother, leaving me to drive back alone.

At four in the morning, I woke up. I don't know why, but something felt strange. I looked out of the window. On the other side of the street I saw a cat, cowering in the entrance of a house. Then someone knocked at my door. I opened and Xenia was standing in front of me.

'I wanted to be with you, Max.'

'Is Natasha OK?'

'Yes. Absolutely.'

She came in and started undressing, taking her wet shoes off, sitting down. I took her feet into my hands.

They were cold. I pulled the socks off and rubbed her feet to warm them up.

'How did you get here?'

'I was reading in the kitchen when I heard our neighbour leaving and remembered that he always drives to work early. He gave me a lift.'

I kissed her foot and then her hands.

'I told Babka about us,' Xenia said, lying on her front, looking at me.

'What do you mean?' I caressed her naked shoulders.

'What happened between us.'

'Christ.' I felt embarrassed and sensed my face was turning red. 'How did she, I mean, what did she say?'

'Not much. She was silent and I guess didn't take it well. But eventually she said that as long as I was happy, she'd be happy. You know she likes you. And she's still amazed that you came to look her up. And that you had the guts to shoot that fucker. In a way, she admires you. And so do I, by the way,' she added.

'But,' I tried to say.

'No comment,' Xenia quickly interrupted.

Jazz

The next two weeks passed and I did not seem to notice, though I had always had a very precise feeling for time, which went for me hand in hand with responsibilities, deadlines, work. The factor time was essential in most crimes and many criminals ended up behind bars because of time. Wrong time, inconsistency, not enough time, too much time. Now time had lost its meaning. It floated by, or, maybe, it was static whilst my life was drifting past. When you are in love, time ceases to exist. Mischa did not call and did not return my calls either. I went every day to the Conservatory and listened to Xenia play. Beethoven, Kunst der Fuge, Berg, Ravel, Liszt. In between, I spent hours reading at the Café Scriabin and after a while the waiters knew me too and greeted me like a friend when I dropped in alone.

One evening, we were coming back late to the hotel, the bar was already half empty and the pianist was packing up. Xenia sat down at the piano and started playing jazz.

'Hey, listen to this. I've got this from an Oscar Peterson CD.' And she started playing. Soon the drummer got up from the couch and started accompanying her.

'What is it you're playing?'

'Blues of the Prairies,'' the drummer said with a broad

American accent, swinging back and forth with the rhythm.

'Let's play Gershwin's Summertime, she suggested to the drummer. I sat down and ordered Armagnac for her, the drummer and me. Xenia sipped it whilst continuing to play with her left hand. The bar was starting to fill up again as people were coming back to the hotel.

'I didn't know you could play jazz,' I said when we left the bar half an hour later. She put her arm around my shoulder.

'I guess there are a lot of things you don't know about me. Like my paintings.'

'Well, I've seen them. Some of them.'

'Where?'

'Your grandmother showed some to me. The ones which you keep next to your old piano. And I saw the one at Oleg's place. The one in blue, a very powerful blue.'

'Yes,' she said, looking pensive. 'I think I liked that one best. I painted it when I visited him. Right there and then. And I'll show you some more, new ones. I keep them at a friend's studio.'

As we stepped out of the lift, I turned to her. 'Talking of your blue painting, do you know why your grandmother doesn't talk to her brother anymore?' I got out the key and opened the door to our room.

'Yes. Sure. I mean, I think I know,' Xenia said as we sat down. 'First, there was the war and they lost contact. After the war, Babka went to live in Moscow, not wishing ever to go back, but he stayed on. You know, when he was old enough to understand, he resented her for having a child fathered by a German.' She looked at me, almost pleadingly: 'You must understand. I don't know how he was when you found him. But he's changed a lot during the last years. Straight after the war, he was very disturbed and spent many years locked up. I'm not sure whether that helped him or caused even more damage. I do know that Babka visited him over there in the looney bin and, what can I say, it became very ugly between them.'

'Hmm. But now he seems OK?'

'Well, I spent a week with him, and he seemed OK. But he is under very heavy medication. Did you not notice his speech? It's slurred and there are words he can't pronounce.'

'I thought it was because of the vodka.'

'Probably that too. I never drank as much as during those days I spent with him. Maybe that's the reason why I painted so well.' She stopped to think.

'So, one day I decided to visit him. Babka told me not to go. I think she was afraid that he might become violent, as he had when she visited him. But he was actually really nice.' She paused again.

'You know, it's weird what war does to you. He became crazy and, sadly, hated his sister for getting raped by a Nazi. Instead of pity, he felt just hatred, as if it was her fault. True, she ran away, but I didn't understand him. And we couldn't talk about it either. Whenever I tried, he just walked out into the garden pretending to get some wood or whatever.' She remained silent for a while, thinking. 'But he was kind to me. And so I painted that painting for him.'

'Which he loves. It's extraordinarily beautiful. Really.'

'That's kind of you to say.' We lay down on the bed without undressing. Her embrace was warm and gentle, but she was asleep before I could kiss her.

Natasha's secret

Two days later I waited in front of Natasha's factory in gloomy rain. She had asked to see me and I was nervous. Rows and rows of workers were leaving through the main gate. This used to be a workers' paradise, but none of the workers seemed too happy, even though they were leaving the morning shift – early in the evening. Then I saw her. No, in fact, I didn't recognise her straight away, but she was the only one smiling and chatting.

'Natasha!' I shouted across, making my way through the rows of exiting workers.

'Max. Good evening. So nice of you to come and pick me up.' She must have caught me gazing at her clothes, as she added, 'Sorry about my outfit, though. I know it's not very fashionable.' I felt embarrassed.

'No need to be sorry, Natasha. It's nice to see you,' I said. We got into the Jeep and drove back.

'Come up and have a cup of tea whilst I change. Go to Xenia's room and wait there.' I felt like a schoolboy about to be punished. At least, I felt my conscience. What was Natasha going to say? She had all the right to be furious with me for going out with her daughter's daughter. I was wondering what was going on in her head. I took the glass and sat down in Xenia's armchair. Her paintings were still in a pile next to her piano. To distract myself, I looked at them again. There were some drawings of people and a number of abstract oil paintings. Blue dominated in each painting. Natasha came in and urged that we go to the restaurant straight away. The silence in the car felt stifling.

Natasha chose to sit inside. It was dark but with a pleasant atmosphere, dark blue walls and equally dark blue curtains. We ordered, that is, Natasha ordered for me too, whilst I chose the wine.

'I needed to talk to you, Max.' Natasha said once the waiter had gone. 'It's about Xenia.'

Almost instinctively I tensed up.

'Actually I need to talk about two issues. The first one is your relationship. You know I like you. No, like is not the right word, it's more than just like and not only because of what you did so many years ago. But I have to admit I am struggling with the fact that you are going out with Xenia. She is my granddaughter. She could be yours, Max. How can you do this to us.'

Natasha looked down, biting her lip. I did not know what to say as I felt rotten.

'I'm not saying this because Xenia is a child. She is not. She is a tough cookie and you are certainly not the first man in her life. But I was so shocked and, in a way, saddened and angry as I felt betrayed by you. You were my hero and then you did that? Given your age, I think it is wrong.'

Again she paused. Again, I remained silent, not knowing how to defend myself. Xenia initiated this, not me. I tried to flee. She is a grown-up. She knows. Thoughts were shooting through my head. In the end I simply said:

'Natasha. I tried not to have this happen, but I cannot help it. I love her. It may sound pathetic coming from an old man like me, but I really truly do.'

She glanced at me, trying to gauge my honesty and smiled vaguely and said, 'you know, in Soviet times you learn not to struggle against things you cannot change. I cannot forbid you to do what you are doing. And Xenia explained. Explained that it was her who pushed you whilst you, in a way, pushed her away. So we argued and she got very angry and told me she didn't need a father figure but loved you because she understood you whilst she didn't understand her fellow students or all the other previous boyfriends. And still I was angry. And I do not approve.'

She started eating as soon as the food arrived. I was wondering what was going on in her head as she preferred to eat in silence. I felt saddened as I felt a closeness and connection to Natasha that was not reciprocated. It was only when we had finished eating that she picked up the conversation again.

'Actually, that's not what I wanted to talk to you about,' she said, as if continuing her last sentence twenty minutes later. 'It's about me, not Xenia. And about what happened. About him...' she hesitated obviously struggling, but then continued, looking straight in front of her, 'the man who raped me.'

'He's dead.'

'Well, no,' Natasha said awkwardly. 'One of them you killed. But the other one survived, as far as we know.'

'But,' I tried to interject. 'He didn't...' I could not say "he didn't rape you" straight into her face. I looked at her. Her face had become cold and distant, her eyes concentrating on a point on the opposite wall.

'Yes. That's right. He wasn't when you shot them. But,' she looked down and her hands grabbed the serviette, crunching it into a tight ball. 'But the other one had raped me first. He had raped me with such brutality that I remember it as if it happened yesterday. I hardly remember the second one, the one you killed.'

I nodded.

'The one you killed didn't rape me. But the first one did, whatever he was called.'

'Müller,' I said.

'Maybe, Max. But I actually don't care what he was called as I don't want to remember his name. Thank God I don't recall his face. But I remember the hoarseness of his hands beating and then groping me, his filthy breath, his groaning when he finally finished. The feeling of wet filth and disgust. And thank God you shot the other one. Just in time before also he could rape me.'

She stopped and her words slowly sunk in. But rather than leaving the conclusion to me, she quickly added, 'so the one you shot was definitely not the father. But the other one, Müller, was my daughter's father. And he is still free and may be walking around somewhere.'

'Or dead.'

'No. I don't think he's dead. I have a sense that he's still alive. Out there. Somewhere.'

She stopped and looked at the wall in silence for a long time, thinking, then gulping down her glass of wine and refilling it herself without waiting, without looking up. I finished my glass too.

'Max. I told you as I thought you need to know,' Natasha continued. 'Because of Xenia. You are the person closest to her and I sense despite all my anger and opposition she won't drop you.' She observed the waiter refilling her glass and took a long sip. 'But she doesn't know. She wants to know, as she was probing the other day. But I cannot tell her. It's too painful for me to tell this to her. And Oleg doesn't know either. Nobody knows, except you and me.'

'And Müller.'

She nodded. 'And Müller'.

We continued drinking in silence, as I was taking in what she had said. I felt bitterness in my stomach and anger about myself. We left the restaurant in silence. When I drove her home, a fine rain was falling and I felt as if the sound of the windscreen wipers allowed us not to talk.

Back at the hotel I sat in the bar, listening to the pianist playing hotel music. I still had this feeling of bitterness as memories came flooding back. The waiter brought me a glass of Armagnac in a big cognac glass. It was Georgian Armagnac, biting and yet sweet, different from the one he had served me before. I tried to concentrate my mind but could not get the thought out of my head of Müller strutting around in Russia in his uniform. Natasha was probably right. He could very well still be alive and at large.

Müller had tried to kill me, and now I knew that he was the only one who had raped Natasha.

But then I had to think. Why did she tell me this? Why did I have to know? She had tried to block it out of her life and now that I appeared, she had to bring it up – in the context of her disapproval of my feelings for Xenia.

I needed another glass of Armagnac. The pianist started playing Brazilian jazz. I lit a Cohiba and decided to track Müller down and bring him to justice. *Alea iacta est*, and it was Natasha who had cast the dice.

Mischa

It was midnight when I managed to reach Mischa again.

'Where are you Max? Are you OK? No news from you for ages.'

'I'm OK, Mischa. I'm still in Moscow. Tried to call you many times. Got stuck here.'

'Stuck? What do you mean? With the Jeep?'

'No, of course not. Don't worry. Nothing to do with your Jeep. Everything's fine. But, tell me first of all, how are you?'

'Fine, Max, just fine.'

'Mischa, you are lying. I can hear it in your voice.'

'No, Max, I really am fine. I said I'd call you if I were not.'

'What did the tests say?'

'Nothing much, anyway. I guess you are enjoying yourself in Moscow?'

'Mischa,' I said. 'I need your help.'

'Go ahead.'

'You remember, when we were there where I shot Moser?'

'Yes. Of course I do…'

'Mischa. Who was the other guy? Müller. The other SS shit. And do you remember the name of their friend, the other guy, you know, the one from the station.' Mischa remained silent for a while. 'Why?' He broke the silence. 'Why do you want to know?'

'Please don't ask, Mischa. I just need to know.'

'Have you met the girl?'

'Girl? Oh, yes, I mean, she is in her sixties. I've met her. A couple of times, in fact, and we've talked about things.'

'Also about?'

Now it was my turn to hesitate.

'Yes, Mischa,' I said. 'We came too late. When we got there, she had already been raped by Müller.'

'By Müller?'

'Yes, Mischa, by Müller. I know I should have killed him.' I paused. 'What was his first name?'

'Walter. Walter Müller.'

'Any idea where he was from?'

'Rhineland?'

I paused. There was no chance of finding a Walter Müller, even if he lived in Rhineland. I bet there were at least five thousand Walter Müllers in Rhineland.

'Do you remember the name of Müller's friend? The guy who knocked me out at the station?'

'No. Let me think.'

He remained silent for a while.

'I honestly can't remember his name,' he said in the end. 'Sorry. But, when are you back, Max?'

'Don't know. Mischa. It's silly, I know. No, it's not silly, but it may sound silly: I've met someone.'

'You? I thought you were going to become a Buddhist monk.'

'Very funny.'

'Seriously, Max. I've never met anyone as disinterested in women as you,' Mischa laughed. 'Well, it had to happen now that you're retired. Who, if I may ask?' he added.

'Someone related to Natasha.'

'Her daughter?'

'No, actually, her granddaughter.' There was silence at the other end of the line.

'Max, you must be joking,' Mischa finally said quietly.

'No, it's true.'

There was silence again. I literally could hear Mischa think. Finally he said, 'Are you out of your mind to go off with the granddaughter?'

'I just, well, I guess it just happened.'

'Max, you are 65. That's sick.'

'I know,' I heard myself answer. 'I don't know how it happened, Mischa, but it happened. In the beginning it came more from her, but then it really hit me.'

'Max. Wake up. You are such a perv. What are you doing?'

'But,' I suddenly had a thought, 'Pablo Casals was 35 years older than his father in law when he got married the last time.'

'I don't care about Casals. He was a bloody musician. You are a judge. You should know about vulnerable kids – what are you doing? Going off with one? Look, Max, let's talk about this when you are back,' Mischa said. 'I've always trusted your judgement, but here you're mad. Irresponsible. Max. Are you listening?'

'Yes.'

'You're in your bloody midlife crisis because you hate your retirement.' He turned quiet and just added: 'You have to stop this, Max. And please don't hurt her.'

'I won't hurt her, Mischa.'

'She must be very disturbed if she is going out with you of all people. There's something seriously wrong with her. Sorry to be so blunt.'

'Hmm...' I paused.

'Talk another time. Got to go.' I could hear Mischa's anger over the phone. I had never heard him talk like that before. He hung up.

I felt devastated. My best friend condemning me for being in love.

I woke up the next morning and Mischa's words were still swirling around in my head. Mischa was right. Yes, of course he was right, but what could I do. Flee? I tried that. Retreat into my shell? No, I knew I was past the point of no return. Actually, I felt that I was doing the right thing, being in love. And then again, Mischa made it sound as if I was a criminal who knows it is wrong but who still cannot stop himself from committing a crime. On pure reason there is only one thing I could now do: run and bury my thoughts hoping to forget. Hoping not to be found. But then again, I was no longer pure reason.

I had to think of something else, otherwise I would go insane. Thank God and more importantly, Walter Müller is now the immediate task. How would I find Walter Müller?

Searching for Müller

Killing Karl Heinz Hempe had been easier than I had imagined it to be. No bad conscience. Closing a chapter that needed to be closed and that could not be closed otherwise. In a way it was strange, though, as I am a person with a relatively well-developed conscience. I often had questions after sending criminals to jail, when, knowing that I had done the right thing, I still questioned afterwards whether I had not erred in my decision about the length of the sentence, whether the twelve years I had sent someone to jail for were really justified. Sometimes I erred on the side of leniency. I knew that some of my Bavarian colleagues would have given a case fifteen years, without question. On other occasions, I had asked myself afterwards whether the fifteen years behind bars I had condemned someone to had been too harsh.

Still, I reflected back after judging and executing Hempe that, after the war, I had sworn to myself never ever to kill again. I had killed in the war and it was horrible. I often had to think about those soldiers who were like us, most of them kids, taken straight from school, with young and innocent faces. I sometimes cried, not only when my friends got killed but also when we had killed Soviet soldiers. I personally had difficulty seeing those kids as my enemies. They weren't. We were their enemies, but they were not mine.

When the war was over and I ended up in prison camp, a deep sadness overwhelmed me and I felt pain, and suffered for the people I had killed and grieved for the fifty million people whom the war had claimed. Why had I been spared? My friends often prayed, but I could not as I knew, my prayers would not be answered. Prayers never are, particularly prayers of the losing side during war or from a prisoner of war camp. The only thing I felt like praying for was forgiveness. But also that I could not do as I felt it was not up to the God, who could have prevented all of this, to forgive. I thought God should ask us for forgiveness. Forgiveness for letting all of this happen. Forgiveness for not stopping the war, the madness, the Holocaust. Alas, he never did.

In my case, I felt it was up to the women whose husbands and children we had killed.

I felt that my five years in camp were fully justified but later had to ask: what happened to all those who committed 'real' crimes, who erased villages, raped, bombed, who supported Nazism.

Back in Germany, I realised that the Nuremberg trials had only dealt with a few cases. The vast majority of Nazis lived on, many SS murderers, as if nothing had happened. Many of the Nazi machine had been integrated into the new German bureaucracy. How many judges got disqualified?

I decided, like so many of us, to close my mind and to move on once I had returned and concentrate on my studies in Munich and then on my work. I loved living in solitude to be able to think, be it the solitude of our university library or the solitude of mountains, with Julia.

Walter Müller. I needed to find Walter Müller but had no clue how to track him down. I needed to find someone who knew him or who had known him. But I had forgotten the name of his SS friend. Then it struck me: I needed to get back home to look at my war diaries, which I knew were up there stacked away in the attic. There I knew I would find the name of Müller's friend. If I could track him down, I reckoned he would take me to Müller.

Maxims

Why had I not thought of my diaries before? Why did I not take them along on this trip? I had not even seen them when I recently cleaned up the attic. Just before lunch I drove to the Conservatory hoping to find Xenia there. I could hear Chopin as I was walking down the corridor. The Mazurka. I stopped and listened to the melancholy tune till she had finished playing and entered the room.

Xenia was sitting in front of her piano, eyes closed, concentrating. I was hoping that she would start playing again, but she opened her eyes and got up when she saw me. We hugged and kissed.

'God, Max, you smell of booze. What did you have for breakfast?' She laughed disarmingly.

'Muesli and Cognac.'

'You taste disgusting,' she laughed.

'Thanks.' I said. 'I'll have to go back to Germany.'

'I know,' she said. 'I sensed you were going to go. But I'm OK with it now.'

'Hmm.'

'So, when are you off?'

'Probably tomorrow morning.'

'And will you come back one day?'

'Xenia. Of course I'll be back.'

'Don't worry, Max, I never doubted,' she said.

'In fact, I'm going to leave Mischa's car here and take a plane, so that I can fly back and be back sooner.'

'Can I drive it?'

'Well, why not. It's downstairs.'

'Let's go for a walk.'

We left the Conservatory and drove to the Lenin Hills. I looked at Xenia from the side: she drove like Mischa, I thought, her right hand casually on the steering wheel, the left elbow stuck out of the window. She squeezed the Jeep between two cars and we got out. The sun was amazingly intense and the air was warm. Children were playing in the park. We bought ourselves a massive ice cream each and sat down in the grass.

'Why do you need to go back to Germany now?'

I knew this question was going to come and had decided to be as truthful as possible, without breaking Natasha's secret.

'I want to read something in my diaries. I feel there are some missing pieces, which I have not found out yet, either by speaking with your grandmother or by visiting your uncle.'

She looked for a long time at the clouds and then turned around and glanced at me with dark and serious eyes.

'I know what you want to find out. You need to know, how to find the other SS creep who was present when my grandmother got raped. And who you shot but didn't kill. Müller.'

I was taken aback. How did she know? Had she talked to her grandmother? I did not want her to know what I was doing in Germany, as I did not want to burden her with the past. That was my past. And Natasha's past, not Xenia's, even though Xenia was a product of that past. I looked at her from the side and then lay down in the grass. Xenia bowed over me so that her hair was touching my face.

'Don't say anything, Max. No need to explain. Not now. But, maybe, you can talk about it when you're back. Whenever that will be', she added after a while.

Again, Mischa's words crossed my mind. But no, I was not insane being in love with Xenia.

In the restaurant of the hotel, we were the only guests. Xenia took her dessert plate with her to the bar and sat down at the piano.

'This is my farewell to you,' she said, and started playing the first three of Chopin's Etudes opus 25. Then she started Chopin's Mazurka op 63 No 3, which she knew I loved. To me it sounded particularly sad the way she played it. She got up once she had finished and came over to my armchair, pulling me gently to my feet. She held me for a long time in her arms, stroking my head and then looked into my eyes.

'I don't like parting, Max. That's why I'm not staying overnight. So, farewell. But please come back soon. I'll miss you.'

'I will.'

'I know you will.' We kissed and stayed embraced for a long time and then she put her fingers into my pocket and pulled out the car keys.

'Poka.' She turned around and swiftly walked towards the door. There she waved a quick good bye and was off.

I walked back to my room, which seemed strangely empty. The next morning I left my luggage with the concierge and made my way to Sheremetyevo. I had to think back to my previous trip to the airport. The taxi driver had been right. Again, I had nothing to check in and went straight through to the gate. In the early evening I was back at home.

I went up to the attic and, after some searching, found it. 'Maxims.' My thought-book from the front. I had not touched it for ages. With hindsight it seemed like a miracle that I managed to keep it on me during the war, in the field hospital, in camp. I remember when we arrived in camp, all our stuff was taken from us. Including my thought-book. I got it back, trading in a golden girl's necklace which Karsten, my fellow comrade in the field hospital, had given me in one of his last moments of consciousness as he was dying on the stretcher next to me. I did not need the gold necklace but needed my thought-book to survive. It seemed thinner than I remembered. Some of the pages stuck together when I tried to open them. Carefully, I pulled them apart and started browsing. Soon I had found what I was looking for on page 58.

A week later. We are still in Ukraine. For days we haven't moved. But for days we haven't been attacked either. Where is the Soviet Army? The quietness is eerie and we suspect that they are regrouping somewhere in the marshes, miles ahead, days from us, at the same time we are awaiting the arrival of another tank brigade. We take the time to play cards, to joke, to wash. Some of us are writing home. When I say "Us", I mean the Wehrmacht, the regular army. That's us. I have to differentiate as there is also the Waffen SS. Himmler's elite army who don't know an arse from an elbow. We don't mix. Our brigadier doesn't want us to mix. He hates them. I don't know why they consider themselves an elite. They aren't fighting better. Their loss rate is higher. They don't think. They are renowned, though, for their brutality and part of their mission is 'cleaning up': Jews, communists, gypsies. In each town they round them up and transport them away. By now we know where: to concentration camps. We know – we are not naïve. So that is the country we are fighting for. A country that sends people with different beliefs, weltanschauungen or skin colour to slave away in concentration camps. Mischa, Tom, Martin, I – we all are disgusted.

Yesterday Mischa and I went to the station to pick up Klaus who was re-joining us after three months in field hospital. The platform was full of people in shabby clothes, the men and women separated. Some had swollen faces and blood on their clothing. In between them marched the SS, including Lieutenants Müller and Odenbrecht.

Odenbrecht. That was him. Now I remember. Odenbrecht. I figured if I could find him, I would be able to track down Müller too. Fascinated, I continued reading as the picture of the station with all those people came back into my mind.

I had seen the two a couple of times. Fucking creeps. Müller was the one with the big mouth, probably just around 25, I guessed. Odenbrecht was probably barely 24. They were strutting up and down the platform, hissing orders at the men and women whose faces expressed fear, apathy or, where there was no fear, hatred. We noticed how they quickly passed those people who were full of hatred and stopped, stared and sometimes hit those who were panic-stricken in the first place. Despite the fact that there were well over one hundred people, the platform was dead quiet, except for their shouting or the noise of their boots on the stones of the platform.

Suddenly we heard a small voice crying. The tiny voice of a child. Müller and Odenbrecht turned around, 'Where is the child' Müller shouted. He went barking and pulling at the people until he had found it. He grabbed the child, who was by now crying in panic. The father clung on to the child. 'Let the stupid git go, you rotten parasite,' Müller hissed. But the father held on to his son, pleading with Müller. Müller took a step back, hesitant about what to do. Would he give in? He? The SS officer? No way. His word was the order everyone had to obey. He pulled out his gun and hit the father over the head. Once. Twice. The father collapsed. There was blood coming from his head, his nose, his mouth. His eyes seemed frozen. The child cried, whilst Müller cracked open the father's head with the butt of his gun.

I don't remember what came over me, but I jumped at Müller and hit him as hard as I could under the chin against his neck. He broke down immediately. I watched him lie on the floor with a feeling of deep satisfaction, but then, out of no-where, came a blow which landed just under my ear almost dislocating my jaw. It hurt like hell. I just had enough time to look around to see Odenbrecht's fist coming for the second blow, which hit my left eye. I stumbled backwards and my head knocked the ground. Then I blacked out.

The next thing I remember was that Mischa was pulling me away from it all. He dragged me back to our unit. The next day we went on the offensive again – and the SS troops were gone.

Mischa told me a few days later when our offensive had stalled and we were sitting by the trench in the rain that Uwe Odenbrecht had shot and killed the father and when the child didn't stop screaming, he had also killed the child with a single shot between the eyes. As Mischa was around, Odenbrecht had not dared to shoot me too.

When Mischa walked away, I started crying, and cried for hours. I don't know. I had killed people. I saw some people, I think, I had killed. Young soldiers with white and innocent faces. But I killed them because they were advancing towards me, ready to kill me and I did not want to die. But I never killed a civilian and never will kill a civilian, let alone a child, with a shot between the eyes. It's so insane. Where has this world come to and why am I part of this world?

What goes on in the minds of those SS swine who are out there killing people just because they don't want to let go of their children. And I think that there is no logical answer. Some of my friends simply repeat what others say, 'it's war' and that 'things are different in war'. But I am a soldier, and, yes, things are different, of course. But, still, neither I nor any of my comrades or commanders walk about rounding up innocent people, shooting them.

Reading this again, I had to ask myself the same questions, as I had not found an answer yet. There was no answer. But Walter Müller and Uwe Odenbrecht were both probably still alive. And I knew what I had to do.

It was early in the morning when I left my apartment. It was a strange feeling, walking the streets that I used to every day. I exchanged a few words with my newspaper agent, bought the *Sueddeutsche Zeitung* and the *International Herald Tribune*, walked to my baker and bought croissants and some bread and coffee, yoghurt, fruit, jam, honey at my local Spar supermarket.

'You look absolutely relaxed, Herr Doktor. I've never seen you like that – where were you on holiday?'

I was slightly taken aback. There was a mirror on the wall, and, looking at the person staring at me, she was right: I saw the formerly grumpy judge, wearing jeans and a black polo shirt, looking relaxed and tanned.

'I retired, Frau Sellmayer.'

'What,' she exclaimed. 'You? I thought you'd never retire. But you're far too young.'

'Not quite, but I'm getting younger,' I said.

'Well, one can see that. But tell me, Herr Doktor, where did you go?' she insisted.

'Actually, I went to Russia and spent some time in Moscow.'

'Amazing, well, I'm glad you're back. And we'll see you now every morning, won't we?' she concluded, turning to the next customers who had been waiting.

I rushed home and dialled Mischa's number whilst munching on my croissants. Mischa came to the phone immediately and said he remembered Uwe Odenbrecht, now that I mentioned his name. Of course.

'But, more importantly,' he added laughing, 'where's my Jeep?'

'I left it with Xenia. Sorry.'

'What's that supposed to mean?'

I paused, and then said, 'Don't worry, I'll buy you a new one.'

'I don't need a new one. I just want my old one back.'

'Sorry, Mischa, I think it will always stay on in Russia.'

'You're joking, Max?'

'Nope. Don't worry, we'll settle that later.'

'Tell me, what happened to Xenia? Have you woken up?'

'No, Mischa. She is,' I paused to think, 'she is serious. And I'm serious. Look, I don't want to talk about it over the phone. But tell me more about Odenbrecht. What do you remember about him?'

Mischa remained quiet for a while.

'Not much. Waffen SS. He hit you and knocked you out.'

'I know. Haven't forgotten.'

'Well, he was probably 23 or maximum 25-years-old. So maybe about 70 by now. Think he was from Bonn. He was a close friend of Müller's. The funny thing is, I think he was a carpenter too. Not sure anymore who told me though, but, you know, maybe only Müller was a carpenter, not both of them. But who cares, Max?'

'I do.'

Again, he turned silent. I looked out of the window,

where a group of children were now walking down the street. I had to get back to reality.

'Max. You know, this is history. Don't go back. Really. Too much water has flown under too many bridges,' Mischa said.

'Don't know, Mischa. We'll see. You know the book's still open. There was never any justice, Mischa. If Odenbrecht and Müller simply went home after the war and life continued just like normal, then the book is still open,' I said.

'Yes, I know, Max. Not just this book, whole bloody libraries are still open. But it's not your job to close books. Either you live in the past or in the future. You are already hurting her, simply flying from Moscow to Munich. Isn't she the future? Why bother about the past.'

'Because it's there.'

'Because it's there. Sure. But there are too many things that are still "there".'

'Yes. But this one concerns me. And in some ways also Xenia. Particularly Müller.'

'Max. I closed the Odenbrecht chapter for you. I punched him and made sure he didn't shoot you.'

'What you punched him? You never told me.'

'No need to tell you. I think he would have shot you, had I not punched him.'

'You knocked him out?'

'No, I didn't punch him hard enough. But I told him I would shoot him if he did anything to you. So the chapter is closed. I closed it for you, Max.'

I realised all of a sudden that I had not even asked Mischa about his health – and Mischa had only enquired about his Jeep.

'Look, Mischa, let's talk about more important things. How are things with you? I mean, any other results? Tests?'

'Well,' Mischa said after a pause, 'I didn't really want to talk about it, but for the last two weeks I've been dizzy every day. And memory loss. Sometimes I cannot speak properly. Not now, but sometimes.'

'What? And you are telling this to me now? Mischa, why didn't you call me? Damn it, Mischa, this is ugly. Have you seen a specialist?'

'No, but this week I'll get a scan, and stuff.'

'Shit.'

'You don't say.'

Suddenly I felt mean and awful. Here was Mischa, my best friend, in deep trouble, and I was doing what?

'When is the scan?'

'Thursday.'

'I'll be there.'

'That would be great,' he said and added: 'I need to go now. So see you Thursday.'

'Yep. Definitely. See you then.'

I hung up and went to the kitchen to make myself another espresso. I was upset. I did not want to believe that Mischa might be seriously ill. What could I do to help him? My thoughts were drifting back to our trip to the Soviet Union. He seemed alright then.

Odenbrecht and Müller came back to my mind. Would

they still be alive? Karl Heinz Hempe had been. Mischa was. I was. Why shouldn't they be? The mere thought made me angry.

I went to the Englische Garten and sat down on a bench, watching the river flow past, stuffing my pipe. I realised that I had not smoked for a while. The water was flowing fast, it was clear and when I put my hand into it, I was surprised how cold it was. Many years ago, I used to swim in this river with Julia, who loved drifting down the river, being pulled by the current. I sat down on the bench again and relit my pipe, looking at the smoke as it reluctantly rose towards the branches of the trees.

Odenbrecht should be easy to track down. It wasn't a name like Müller. I knew that I needed to track down Odenbrecht first and from him I would find out where Müller was living.

The tobacco was too dry and the pipe did not burn properly. I decided to chuck it away and quit smoking. At least pipe smoking. I tossed it into the river. It was weird to see the pipe bobbing up and down in the fast-flowing water, like a fish.

Odenbrecht

I took the tram to the main post office and started searching through telephone books. Bonn. Odenbrecht. There were quite a few – a hopeless task. I decided to call the first U. Odenbrecht, just to see what happened.

'Odenbrecht,' answered a cheerful woman on the other end.

I hesitated. 'Eh... could I speak with Uwe Odenbrecht please.'

'Sorry, you have the wrong number.' She hung up.

I was glad she did as I did not feel like continuing the conversation with 'Good morning. Do you know whether your father Uwe was in the Waffen SS.'

That was the only Odenbrecht with a first name starting with a U.

I called the next Odenbrecht. R. Odenbrecht. A little boy answered. Next was a man who sounded young. That was no way forward. So he did not live in Bonn anymore. Koblenz. Nothing. Trier, nothing. Koeln, Duesseldorf, nothing. I looked for hours and called twenty-five Odenbrechts in the hope of finding the right one. I was ready to give up when I had not found an Uwe Odenbrecht in Frankfurt and decided to go home. But then I realised I had not checked either Wiesbaden or Mainz. No U in Wiesbaden but Mainz had one. A carpenter, which was intriguing. Uwe Odenbrecht. Carpenter. That must be him, I thought. Was he that easy to find? I decided to call him and he picked up the phone.

'Odenbrecht'.

I did not recognise his voice.

'Uwe?'

There was silence at the other end of the line.

'What do you want?' he finally said.

'Are you the Uwe who was born in Bonn?'

Silence again and then he hung up. Definitely the voice of a very old man. What's the point talking to him, he would never tell me over the phone that he had been in the Waffen SS. I had to risk it by visiting him unannounced. I returned home and went to my study where I had kept a pistol, a Heckler & Koch, hidden in the secret drawer of my desk. I had bought it illegally ages ago, when I felt threatened by someone whom I had jailed years before and who had threatened to kill me once released. The day of his release had come but nothing ever happened and so I had never used it. The metal was cold and reassuringly heavy. I cleaned it thoroughly of any traces of finger-prints.

Early the next morning I took the train to Mainz.

I arrived in Mainz before lunch and decided to have a pizza at the station restaurant. The pizza was superb, with delicious cheese and fresh Thyme. I looked around the restaurant for something to read and saw a pile of newspapers. I took the first one – *Mainzer Tagesspiegel* and opened the local pages. There were elections for the city council of Mainz and all parties had advertisements and articles. Faces were looking at me: a thirty-year-old housewife, teacher at a primary school, candidate for the Social democrats. A cool looking lawyer for the Liberals. And... I had to swallow: I recognised the nose, the lips: Uwe Odenbrecht, candidate for the Conservatives. He looked into my eyes and asked me to trust him and vote for him. I looked back at him and closed the page and finished my pizza. I preferred to walk the way to Odenbrecht's house in order to avoid leaving too much evidence on the way.

Odenbrecht's house was in an empty, smallish side street in the suburbs. It was rather non-descript, windows with curtains neatly drawn. I rang the bell.

He opened and looked at me with the sort of suspicion you would usually keep for Jehovah's Witnesses. I recognised his face, even after all those years, or maybe just because I had just seen his photo in the paper. He had a prominent nose and rather full lips, which even then, almost half a century later, looked sort of swollen. One of his fingers on his left hand was missing. He was wearing grey woollen trousers and shirt and tie. Mr Biederman at home.

I took off my sunglasses and smiled at him to break the silence which we needed to observe each other.

'Good Afternoon, Mr Odenbrecht,' I said. 'My name is Herbert Frohenhof. I'm from Bremen and was passing through town, visiting some relatives, who advised me to go and talk to you. You know, in Bremen, we'll soon be having local elections too, and I wanted to seek your advice about, well, about how you go about winning votes, when you are our age and conservative.'

'Come in,' he said, rather stony-faced, opening the door. 'I'm sorry, things aren't very tidy.'

We walked down the corridor and through the open door into his living room, which was also his study. The last time the furniture got changed in this room, he probably was less than five-years-old, I thought. Ugly cupboards, heavy, dark wood. A big TV, no books, a few fake looking plants. I tried to look for signs of family but could not see any. Was he married? Nothing seemed to indicate that a woman was living in this household. No family photos, but lots of photos of a younger Uwe with other older men. I turned to the photos. Odenbrecht with local CDU bigwigs. Odenbrecht shaking hands, Odenbrecht speaking at a school and one shaking hands with a grinning Helmut Kohl.

'So you must be pretty busy,' I said, walking towards a chair and sitting down, making sure I would not leave any fingerprints.

'Yes, I've been a councillor for the last quarter of a century, and I'm very busy in the Conservative party.'

'So I can see.' I paused for a moment. 'But how do you deal with the younger generation? How do you convince them to vote Conservative? Most of the youngsters where I live vote Green or SPD.'

'There are always young people who don't know what's right and wrong. Who go demonstrating. Who cause chaos, smoke hashish, don't cut their hair. You may think it primitive, but I simply tell them to get lost, get a job, stop demonstrating. And let the police deal with them. And a lot of kids love to hear it when you tell them about law and order, right and wrong. They don't want that left wing shit.'

'Hmm.' I should have been prepared but these venomous views still surprised me. Nothing had changed since 1945, I thought. I looked along the wall at the photos whilst he was talking. There were some photos which looked older. I got up to take a closer look. There were photos from the war, I suddenly realised. Tanks. Swastikas. I had to swallow, this was all too obvious. But so obviously displayed?

'This was order too?' I pointed at the photos.

'Yes, but that was a different time. Things were right then. But that doesn't mean that they are right today.'

'You mean, what happened then was right?'

'Of course.'

'Well, Mr Odenbrecht, I would have difficulty explaining that to anyone in Bremen.'

'Everything was done in accordance with the law.'

'And the law was right?' Even today, such a view surprised me.

'The law was right. Valid. Passed by the Reichstag, or by decree. Nothing was illegal.'

'But surely, it wouldn't be right today, Herr Odenbrecht?'

'No, Herr...'

'Frohenhof.'

'Herr Frohenhof, of course not. We have different laws today.'

'But the laws then allowed people to kill, just like that?' I looked closely at one photo without waiting for his answer. 'Is that in Ukraine?'

'You seem to know,' he said, slightly taken aback.

'Did you fight there?'

'Ehh, yes. I was in the army.'

'Hmm.' I paused and looked at the other pictures. What I saw was pretty clear – there was no room for misunderstanding. 'No, Mr Odenbrecht, you were not in the army,' I said to him, turning around to look into his eyes. 'You were in the Waffen SS.'

'No. You're wrong.'

At that moment I heard some noise from the kitchen. Slowly the door opened. Shit, I thought, here go my plans. But it was only a small dachshund that appeared and started licking Odenbrecht's leg. I observed him, how he bowed down and caressed the dog which totally ignored me.

'Unfortunately not, Mr Odenbrecht,' I continued. 'First of all, I recognise you in these pictures, and the uniform you were wearing was not army. I was in the army. And, secondly, I remember you well.' I moved a step closer to face him. 'You were cleaning up behind the lines. The last remaining Jews, some partisans.' I observed his face, which had turned ashen. He was sunk in his chair. His dog slowly walked back into the kitchen. I closed the door and listened. Silence.

'It's not true,' he finally stammered.

'It is. Let me jolt your memory a bit, Herr Odenbrecht.'

'No,' he said. 'No. That is the past. I have nothing to do with the past. Get out of here!' he shouted, still ashen faced.

He tried to get up and I put on a glove and took the pistol out of my rucksack.

'Just sit back, Odenbrecht, and listen.'

His hand was shaking. He looked as if he was going to be sick any second. If he threw up now or fainted, it would spoil my plans. If there were anyone in the house, he would have called them by now, I thought.

'I remember this all too well,' I continued with a quiet voice. 'And I cannot imagine that you do not manage to remember this too. Unless, of course, my little experience with you happened to you every single day and so you cannot remember petty details. But for me it was like yesterday.'

I sat back in my chair, keeping my pistol in my lap, observing how he calmed down a bit.

'My friend, he was called Mischa and was a Wehrmacht Officer, and I went to a station in Ukraine to pick up a comrade who was rejoining us after months in hospital. The platform, as I remember in every detail, down to the smell of urine and fear, was full of people in shabby clothes. The men and women had been separated. Some had swollen faces or blood on their clothing. In between them marched Müller and you, Odenbrecht.'

'No, that wasn't me,' he protested.

'Sorry, Odenbrecht,' I said, realizing I was getting angry. I felt like punching him to wake him up. Just punching his ugly nose.

'I do have a pretty good memory,' I said instead, trying to suppress my anger and disgust. 'And I had seen you a couple of times before. Müller was the one with the big mouth. You were strutting up and down the platform, hissing orders at the men and women who were in total panic. Mischa and I noticed how you quickly passed those people who were full of hatred but stopped and sometimes hit those who seemed full of fear. You were such despicable cowards.' I paused to look at my pistol. It calmed me down to feel the neutral and cold metal.

'We were just following orders,' Odenbrecht said. I laughed out loud.

'That's such a stereotypical answer, Odenbrecht.' He opened his mouth again.

'Just shut up and listen,' I shouted at him. He sank back in his chair. 'Anyway,' I continued with a quiet voice, 'even though there were well over one hundred people, the platform was dead quiet, except for your shouting and the noise of your boots on the stones of the platform. Suddenly we heard a small child crying. Müller pulled at the people until he had found it. He grabbed the child, who was crying in panic. The father clung on to the child, pleading with Müller. Don't you remember that scene, Odenbrecht?'

Odenbrecht stared at the wall with a blank expression.

'Would you not hold on to your son, Odenbrecht, when an animal like Müller tries to take him from you?' Odenbrecht continued to stare at the wall. I realized he probably had no children. I felt my stomach was cramping up. 'Well, Müller took a step back, as if hesitant about what to do. But he had to be tough, particularly as you were watching, so he pulled out his gun and hit the father over the head until he collapsed. I don't remember what came over me, but I jumped at Müller and hit him as hard as I could under the chin. He broke down immediately. Then I felt a blow. I just had enough time to look around to see your fist coming for the second blow, which knocked me unconscious.'

I stopped again and looked at Odenbrecht, who was staring speechlessly at me.

'Just don't say "That wasn't me". The next thing I remember was my friend Mischa dragging me back to our unit before you or Müller could shoot me. The next day we went on the offensive again – and you guys were gone. Mischa, however, told me a few days later that you, Odenbrecht, shot and killed the father and when the child didn't stop screaming, you also killed the child with a single shot between the eyes.'

'I... I,' he stammered.

'Yes, you were just following orders,' I interrupted. 'Is this what you're trying to tell me?' He nodded, swallowing.

'That's such bullshit.'

'No, it's true. We had to do it. We had no choice.'

'Bullshit,' I hissed, observing how I got more and more angry with this little pseudo-conservative creep.

'There were no orders to shoot the father. To kill a little child. What had the child done to you? What had the father done?'

'But it was war.'

'So?'

'Things happened in war.'

'No. Things didn't just happen in war. There was no one who asked you to murder that child, to shoot that man. You guys just thought you had the right to treat those humans like vermin. Kill them, as they were low life in your view. You remember Müller, don't you?' He stared at the wall. 'What's happened to Walther Müller?'

'I don't know,' he said, trembling.

'You're lying. I can see you're lying.' I raised the gun and got the silencer out of my rucksack and attached it carefully to the front of the pistol.

'Tell me, where is he?' I aimed the gun at Odenbrecht's stomach.

'I don't, don't know. Really. The last time I heard from him is years ago. Honestly.'

'Where was he then?'

'In the Ticino. In Ascona.'

'Did he live there or was he on holiday.'

'He lives there. He's got a house just outside town, on the hill.'

'Give me his phone number.'

'I honestly don't have it. I have not seen him in years.

Not talked to him. Please don't shoot me. Please. I've done nothing wrong. It was war.'

I was not sure whether he was lying or not, but somehow sensed it could be true. I would be able to track down Müller myself. There can't be that many Müllers living outside Ascona.

'And the child?'

'I'm sorry. Really. But it was war. And we had to round them up. Orders. But I'm sorry. I probably shouldn't have killed the child. Sorry.'

I walked over to his desk and took out some paper and a pen. He was trembling again.

'Sit down over here.' I pointed at the chair. 'And write.'

He got up and went around the desk, taking the pen. He looked at me.

'Write: I was an SS officer during the war.'

He wrote.

'Continue: I killed innocent men, women, children.'

He wrote.

'The only thing I can ask you is to forgive me.'

He hesitated and I lifted my arm, aiming at his head. He wrote.

'Sign,' I said. He signed.

I walked around and stood on his right, reading what he had written.

'An exclamation mark!'

He followed the order. I quickly grabbed one of his kitsch cushions and put it between my gun and his temple. I hesitated a second, and pulled the trigger.

Plop. Like the opening of a bottle of wine, not even champagne. Plop. The bullet went straight through his brain. His head fell forward on to the desk, turning on to the side, where the bullet had entered. His eyes went glazy and expressionless.

I put the gun into his right hand, closed his fingers around the grip and the trigger and went into the kitchen and put some more dog food into the bowl. The dog barely looked up.

The street was empty. I took off my gloves and put them back into my rucksack and put on my hat. At the station I bought Max Frisch's novel *Stiller* and took the train at 16.04 back to Munich.

I was astonished about myself. I was completely relaxed. Again I had killed in cold blood and felt that it was 100% the right thing to have done. I had deliberately stopped the very last moment to reflect whether I should or should not kill. And killed. Odenbrecht had to die. I felt strangely sorry for the dog.

At the same time I think that I might have reacted differently, had he shown remorse. But there was no remorse. Odenbrecht was the same person as in 1944 the only difference being that in today's world, he could not behave the way he behaved in 1944. There was no sense that what he did was wrong. In this respect he was different, very different from all the murderers I had jailed. They all knew that they had done wrong. Some showed remorse, but even those who didn't, knew that they had committed a crime and knew they'd done wrong.

Cancer

I had a weird feeling when I entered my flat, as if someone was waiting for me. I unlocked the door, but found nothing suspicious and, as I checked each room, realised that there was nobody around. I sat down and lit my other pipe, which was a black Dunhill pipe, and poured myself a large glass of Lagavulin. So much for my decision to quit smoking. It was only once I had walked over to switch on my stereo that I realised my answering machine was blinking.

'Max. It's me. Mischa.' I heard his recording as if from afar. 'Look, sorry to disturb you so late. I'm not sure whether you're in bed or around... anyway. Look, Max. I hate to say this, but I had to go to hospital early. Don't worry, I'll be alright.' His voice seemed slurred and there was a pause. Then he continued: 'OK, let me be honest and straightforward. Beep...'

'Oh bummer. Again,' I said realising that the tape had got blocked. I picked up the phone and dialled his home number. His wife Helena came to the phone straight away.

'Max. I'm so glad you called. Mischa is in hospital.'

'Christ, what happened?'

'We don't quite know ourselves, Max. That's what's so awful. You know, he's been feeling sort of dizzy. This morning he fell in the bathroom and was in a really bad state. So I got an ambulance and they took him straight to hospital.' She paused for a moment, reflecting. 'He's better now, and able to talk again, which is a relief.' Helena paused again.

'And? What's going to happen next?'

Her voice sounded composed all of a sudden. 'They did an MRI scan. And they found a tumour in his brain.'

'What? Shit.' I didn't know what else to say. I had to think. 'Helena,' I said. 'Listen, I'm coming tomorrow. First train. I have to see him. This is awful.'

I was shocked and had to sit down. Mischa with a brain tumour. Again, memories of Julia's fight against cancer came up, her frail body, weakened by tumours and treatment. Would Mischa be hit by the same fate? Why? I felt empty and angry with the world.

How long had I known Mischa? Half a century. For half a century we were inseparable friends. I knew him as if he were my alter ego. When we were together, we did not need to talk in order to understand each other. And yet this cancer had escaped me. Shit.

When Julia died, he was with me, as was Helena. Helena and Julia had been close, even though both were very different.

Mischa became a physicist in Stuttgart after the war, having studied physics at Tuebingen university. Helena was a psychologist and had her own private practice, where she treated adults and in the later years, mainly children.

I arrived at 9 the next morning and took a taxi straight

up to the Uhlands Hoehe, where they lived in a somewhat bohemian house with a wild garden and a huge willow tree.

I rang the bell and Helena appeared, looking tired. We embraced.

'Let's go straight to him,' I suggested. She nodded silently and returned into the house to fetch her bag. We got into the taxi which I had kept waiting and drove in silence across town to the hospital.

'I hate hospitals,' Helena said, when we got out.

I also hated hospitals. The smell, the colour of the corridors. The presence of death. We entered and took the lift up to the fourth floor. The building was bright with light shining through the glass roof.

Mischa was alone in a room, sitting on his bed. He looked up when we entered and smiled stoically. Helena embraced him and held him for a long time. I handed him the book *Stiller* by Max Frisch, which I had not read.

'Look,' he said. 'I'm not dying yet. So don't act as if I were. Rather get me something decent to eat, please.' He laughed and his laughter burst the glum atmosphere.

'So, tell me, what did they find?'

'Just a bloody tumour. But it's probably grown recently so that it squeezes some nerves. Hence. Well.' He stopped in mid-sentence.

'You seem to be able to speak properly. Helena said that you were talking rubbish.'

'Please,' Helena said pleadingly.

'Well, I was talking rubbish. And it's actually not fun

when you can't express yourself properly, or when you walk and suddenly the whole world starts moving around you so that you need to sit down on the pavement. You feel like a complete idiot and everyone thinks you're drunk.'

'Rightly so.' He laughed.

'Tell me, what are they going to do? Operate? Chemotherapy?'

'Operate, I guess.'

I had a serious distrust of surgeons. In my view they all just want to operate, cut open, have a look, cut something off, take something out, even if it's not necessary. And they are all terrible prima-donnas who go ballistic if you ask another surgeon for a second opinion.

'He seems OK. Pretty experienced.'

'How old?'

'Your age, I'd say. He's been a brain surgeon for the last twenty years or so.'

'What's his name?' I asked, deciding to double check with my doctor friends in Munich whether the guy was any good.

'Rosenstein.'

'Rosenstein?' It brought back memories. An unusual name.

'You know, I had a class-mate called Wolfgang Rosenstein. His parents were doctors.'

'I'd actually like to talk to Rosenstein,' Helena said.

'He won't tell you anymore than I've already told you,' Mischa said.

'When is the operation?'

'Some time in the next few days, I assume. And,' he looked at both of us, 'I assume you also want to know: the chances are about 60-70 percent of things going well.' He paused and looked at me as if to say, I'm not dying yet.

I left the room to let Helena alone with Mischa. Walking down the corridor, I looked at the doctors who were sitting behind the reception desk, writing things into their files. There was an elderly gentleman, with sparse blonde hair and rimless glasses. I read his name badge. Prof Dr Daniel Rosenstein.

He looked up.

'Max Hardenberg.' I introduced myself.

'Rosenstein,' he said slightly irritated. His eyes were fascinating, blue, with some brown fine circles. They were very clear and warm. Like Wolfgang's I thought.

'Can I help you with anything?' he said.

'Well, yes.' I paused. 'I had a classmate, Wolfgang Rosenstein, and was wondering whether you might be related to him.'

'There are thousands of Rosensteins in this world and I am sorry, but I don't know any Wolfgang.'

I thanked him and walked back to Mischa. I sat down outside Mischa's room waiting for Helena to come out. There was silence and when I entered after waiting for fifteen minutes, Helena was sitting at his bedside, crying. She looked up with red eyes.

'He had to lie down as things started spinning around again.'

I looked at him. He was sleeping peacefully. Helena

wiped her face.

'I guess we have to go through this.' She got up from the bed and came over to the window, where I was standing. I put my arm around her.

'He'll be alright,' I tried to reassure her. 'If the chances are generally 70 per cent, they are closer to 90 for him. He's got this amazing energy, this love for life.'

'I know. Still, it's so hard to see him in this state.'

Schumann

I left them in the late afternoon and returned to Munich, having promised to be back for the operation. We had avoided the topic of Xenia. I felt depressed as deep inside I feared that things might not be going right. I could see it in Mischa's eyes. I had known those eyes for ages. From the days in the trenches over all those years till today. I'd seen this look before, when things were going badly wrong for us. When our friends were getting killed all around us and we only managed to escape by pure luck. I wondered whether Helena could see it or sense it too. She probably could.

The train was gliding through the hilly landscape. I went to the restaurant car and ordered a whisky. It helped. But it also made me realise how much I missed Xenia and that I had not heard anything from her since I left Moscow. As soon as we reached Munich, still at the station, I rushed to a public phone and dialled Natasha's number but only got the answering machine, with Chopin music in the background.

When I opened the door to my apartment, I sensed a presence again. I walked to my living room to check the answering machine, but stopped, realising the door was closed when I had left it open. It was not the day my cleaner normally came. I was not afraid of any burglar and opened the door. I was taken aback. Xenia was sitting on the chaise longue, turning her head and smiling at me with wide eyes.

'I was sleeping, Darling.'

I rushed over as she got up and we embraced in silence. I felt her heart beat against my chest, her hair was ruffled and slightly moist on the side she had been lying.

'This is such a pleasant surprise, Xenia. But what brings you here? And how did you get in?'

She went over to the sofa, sitting down.

'Well, I made a second set of your keys when you were in Russia,' she laughed.

'You really are cheeky. What else did you do? Get yourself a second passport?'

'No, I have plenty of those.' She paused, indicating I should sit down next to her. I sat down on the sofa, taking her hand into my hands, examining the lines.

'I've got a concert the day after tomorrow.'

'Where?'

'Here in Munich.'

'What? Why didn't you tell me?'

'It's a last-minute thing. I'm just filling a gap. Sergej Ivanov was supposed to be the soloist with the Bavaria Radio Orchestra, but he hurt his hand and so he cannot play.'

'And so you got a call from your agent to see whether you'd be willing to jump in?'

'No. I don't have an agent. But I had classes with Sergej and he recommended me to his agent and so I got a call.'

'Amazing. What are you going to play?'

'Schumann. A minor. That's the piece we actually worked on. Sergej is amazing.'

'Hmm. Don't expect me to know it.'

She started whistling the tune.

'Is that the orchestra playing or your piano part?'

'Oh, stop it, you philistine.'

'No. I really don't know,' I laughed.

'OK. I hope you can come along to the concert. I've got you a ticket.' She paused. 'I'm absolutely starving,' she said jumping up. 'I haven't eaten anything for days. An apple and a banana this morning, I think. Your bloody fridge is empty. Typical bachelor.'

'Let's go to a restaurant. Italian or Bavarian?' I said.

'Italian, please. No heavy Bavarian Schweinshaxe or whatever you call it.'

She put her hands around my neck.

'And what have you been up to? Playing golf? Or killing the fucking SS again?'

'Xenia. You know I'm retired.'

'You'll only retire once you've finished your job, Max.' She kissed me gently.

'Maybe you're right,' I said. 'But let's go. I'm starving too.'

We walked down the staircase. Xenia was wearing blue jeans, a bright red pullover and red Converse shoes. She walked lightly, like a ballet dancer. Outside she took my hand.

'Can we walk or do we need to take a cab?'

'It's not far. About five minutes' walk.'

'Great,' she said. The air was fresh and smelled of flowers and grass.

When we entered Sergio's, he came out of the kitchen and looked curiously at Xenia.

'A friend from Moscow,' I said. 'A pianist…'

'I'm Xenia. Bona sera, Sergio.'

'So tell me, what have you been up to?' she turned to me, moving her face closer to mine.

'Not that much. I just spent the day in Stuttgart. Mischa is in hospital.'

'Oh shit. What happened?'

'He's got a brain tumour.'

'Oh fuck.'

'You could say that.'

The waiter, Tonio, came and poured the wine. I looked at the colour. It was beautifully crimson against the candlelight.

'So, what's he going to do? Have an operation?'

'Of course. I guess he has no choice.'

'That's tough,' Xenia said, sipping the wine. 'I'm sorry. I know how much he means to you.'

'Well, his surgeon said that he should be ok. The chances are pretty good for him. He'll pull through.'

'When are you next going to see him?' She looked at me whilst helping herself to some broccoli.

'Tomorrow morning. But tell me, are you going to have a rehearsal before the concert?'

'Of course,' she laughed. 'I don't know them and they don't know me and I don't know the conductor. It's going to be a bit weird. It normally is. But, let me just finish about Mischa. I'd actually like to come along tomorrow, if you don't mind. Do you think that's going to be OK?'

'But you need to practice.'

'No, just the rehearsal. I know my parts inside out.'

'Hmm.' I wasn't sure, how Mischa would react meeting Xenia in hospital.

'Well?' Xenia said, observing me.

'Sorry. Of course it's OK. Not only OK, but I am sure he'd be delighted.'

'Did you tell him about us?'

'Sure.'

'And? What was his reaction?' Suddenly her face showed just a trace of anxiety.

'He was more concerned about his Jeep,' I lied. I just could not tell her about his real reaction. Besides, I wanted her to be unbiased when she met him. One biased side was bad enough.

She laughed and poured me some more wine. 'I just need to be back in the afternoon for the rehearsal,' she said. 'But I guess that shouldn't be a problem.'

'No. I don't expect us to hang around the hospital for hours. Particularly if we take an early morning train.'

'I guess we may have to go over a couple of passages to get things really in sync. Schumann isn't the average Haydn concerto which everyone can play by heart. And the interaction between the soloist and the orchestra needs to be run through a couple of times.'

She finished her glass of wine but declined to drink more.

'And then I have certain ideas how things have to be played. I mean, how certain passages have to be interpreted. And I'm not sure yet whether the conductor will agree and get the orchestra to play things the way I want them played.'

'Can I come to the rehearsal?'

'Not sure I'd want you there. It's like seeing a half-made sculpture or building. It's much better if you see things, I mean, hear things, once they're finished.'

'But I'd like to see you work. I'd like to be there to hear how you and the orchestra study passages. And then, of course, for the finished product.'

'OK. Let me see what I can do.'

The tiramisu arrived and Xenia took a big spoon full, shoving it all into her mouth.

'Tiramisu you have to stuff into your mouth, till there's no space left. Only like that does it taste properly,' she mumbled with her mouth still half full.

I took a big spoonful myself. She was right, the intensity of the flavours was much greater with your mouth completely stuffed. We both continued stuffing ourselves in silence. The moment we finished, Sergio brought a second plate.

'I watched you two. You were like little kids, Dottore. I'm glad you like it.'

When the alarm rang at five a.m., Xenia turned around.

'You know what? I changed my mind. I won't come along. Sorry.'

'Don't worry. You can join one of the next days.'

'Thanks.' She turned around and immediately fell asleep again.

The moment I was about to close the door I heard the telephone ring. I entered again and picked it up. On the other end I could hear Helena's voice in between sobs telling me not to come as Mischa was too unwell to receive anyone.

Outside, the streets were empty, it was too early for people to go to work. I loved walking through the streets early in the morning and remembered many summer days when I walked to court so early in the morning to savour the smells of the awakening city.

Fuck. I was worried about Mischa. This sounded awful and I realised for the first time that he might actually not survive. A brain tumour is awful. Thank God it had not changed his personality. He had kept the clarity of thought and his sense of humour. And yet I feared his reproach which would come when we finally would talk about Xenia.

I still loved her. It was not fake. And she loved me.

The thought of Xenia made me turn around and rush back. I ran up the stairs.

Xenia was reading and drinking coffee. The bitter taste of double espresso calmed me down a bit. Her eyes were sad when I told her about Mischa.

'You have to go and be with him, forget about the concert,' she insisted.

'No, I can't. And what's the point waiting in front of his door. I will go after the concert.'

'OK'.

She had decided to go in the morning to the Herkulessaal, the concert hall, but I joined her only later in the afternoon when the orchestra arrived. They let me sit in the back and listen to the rehearsal. I was amazed to discover a side of Xenia I had not yet got to know. She became stroppy with the conductor when he did not agree with her interpretation. They argued in front of the orchestra. Xenia threatened to walk out, which I thought was rather reckless as there are thousands of unemployed pianists dying to perform in Munich. But in the end, the conductor compromised. And having made him cave in once, it was easy for her to get him to play the whole piece the way she wanted. So much for her fragility, I thought. When they had finished, she got up and walked up to him and shook his hand. She was the only one wearing red plimsolls.

I went to a phone booth and called Helena. Mischa was better but the operation would be delayed by a day. No, she insisted, I should not come and should not talk to him right now. Reluctantly, I hung up. It seemed only days ago that we were driving through Russia, and now this? It's amazing how fast things can turn for the worse, even in peace time. In war, you expect it and it happens all the time, but now? Why?

The concert the next evening was amazing. The Herkulessaal was packed. It is one of the most beautiful concert halls, and the most beautiful one she'd ever played in, Xenia told me. The orchestra started with Coriolan, the Beethoven overture, an amazing interpretation. Then they moved the Boesendorfer grand on to the stage. Xenia entered the hall, dressed in a black silk suit, with a serious face, in full concentration. A faint smile appeared on her lips as she bowed to the audience and shook the concert master's and the conductor's hands. She closed her eyes and started playing in full concentration. The conductor hardly paused in between the movements and seemed to urge the music ahead. Only once the last note had faded away and the audience started its rapturous applause, Xenia finally seemed to be waking up, as if out of a trance. It took her a while to fully get back into herself, but then her face was full of joy. She shook the conductor's and the concert master's hands and waved at the audience. A little boy brought her a huge bouquet of flowers. She kissed him on both cheeks. The audience continued applauding so that she had to reappear three times. At the third time she sat down again. Immediately, the audience quietened down in expectation. She looked at them, as if searching for something and then said with a clear voice:

'Brahms. Ballade. Opus 118. Allegro energico.'

And immediately started playing, fast, furiously. But playing the quiet parts like whispers. When she had finished, she bowed once more. Deep and long. And then disappeared.

I was moved. So that was her, Xenia. I felt humble that she, this amazing pianist, loved me, and felt that the contrasts between her and me, the old philistine, could not have been greater. Everybody got up and walked out for the break. I went out too, looking for Xenia behind the stage and in the crowd but could not find her. When I got back to my seat, she was already sitting in the seat next to mine. No-one seemed to have recognised her as she had changed and was hiding behind dark sunglasses.

We listened to Brahms's third symphony. It was beautiful, particularly the third movement.

'Do you know what?' Xenia whispered into my ear. 'This is the piece I want to have played at my funeral. Not sure whether you'll still be around, though.' She took my hand and pressed it gently. Hers was warm and completely relaxed. I looked at her fingers, at her nails, which she couldn't stop biting, and which nonetheless looked beautiful. Those hands, which could produce magically beautiful music.

I looked at my right hand – the hand that had killed again.

After the concert Xenia was invited to dine with the organisers, the conductor and some other big wigs of Munich's music scene, who I didn't really know. First, I had wanted to go home, but Xenia persuaded me to join. I listened to Xenia and was again surprised about her eloquence. Her English seemed perfect. She really would have made a superb spy. After the main course, I got up and took my glass with me. Xenia glanced over, knowing instinctively where I was going. I sat down in the small and stuffy booth, dialled and took a long sip from the glass. Helena answered. Her voice sounded more relaxed, yet tired. Yes, everything had gone fine, they took out the tumour, stitched him up again. He was conscious and fine when she had left him. She paused. I felt relieved but still did not quite trust the situation.

'Helena. Do you think we can come by and see him tomorrow?'

'He should be OK. Just don't be too early. I'll be there later in the morning too. Probably just before lunch.'

My right hand

Still we managed to get up before seven and rush to the station to take the train to Stuttgart. Plunging into her seat, Xenia said casually: 'So, be honest, Max. When you were alone, did you do any justice stuff? Did you kill anyone?'

I looked around. The first-class carriage was totally empty. Xenia listened silently as I told her the story of Odenbrecht and, once I had finished, she looked at my right hand.

'Last night, you caressed me with this hand, Max. And a few nights ago, this was the hand that pulled the trigger and killed Odenbrecht. I have to admit, it's a bit of a weird feeling.'

She took my right hand into her hands and studied it, following the lines with her little finger.

'I wonder whether Odenbrecht's lifeline was short, sort of truncated. Whether it was written in his hand that he had to die, get killed by you.' I did not reply, and she continued.

'I think it would be quite interesting to check, you know,' she said, studying my lines. 'I think your life line is exceptionally long, do you know that? Mine in contrast,' she showed me the inside of her hands, 'mine seems shorter. Well, relatively.'

'Your hands are longer.'

She slumped back into her seat. The door to the carriage opened at the other end and an elderly man entered and sat down in a seat near the entrance. I looked at Xenia. Her eyes were closed. She stretched out her legs, took off her Converse shoes and put her naked feet on the chair opposite her. With her eyes still closed, she turned her head around, to face me.

'You know, Max. I've been thinking about this. How weird it is, that I love someone who is a murderer. Or maybe just a judge, the ultimate judge, the judge who society does not allow to exist as society does not desire justice as it would be too difficult or too bloody.'

Before I could answer, she continued, 'I don't know. I guess it's a bit presumptuous of me to judge you. All you're doing is taking out those people who committed crimes during the war against others, against humanity and your sister, Julia, Babka. Is that murder? Don't know.'

She stopped and took her feet off the seat.

'But then again,' she continued, 'it's simply wrong to kill these Odenbrechts and Hempes, Max. I mean, Germany doesn't have a death penalty. Should these guys not be brought to justice by the system? Judged by German judges, with the right to defend themselves? If you look at it, Max, you're playing fucking state prosecutor, defence, judge and executioner all in one. It's bloody presumptuous. Literally.'

She sat down again, leaning her head against my shoulder. I knew that she had a point, of course. I turned around to be able to look into her eyes.

'I guess you're right.'

'Oh thank you, Max,' she said.

'No, no. Let me finish please. Let me just explain.'

She briefly looked into my eyes and slumped back in her seat.

'You know, I spent five years as a prisoner of war. Five years is a long time and you know it wasn't a holiday camp. But these five years were important for me. They made me realise what we had done wrong. The crimes we had committed, and I mean not only the SS but, in a way, we all, collectively.'

Xenia sat up with a bolt.

'Oh come on Max,' she said, looking at me. 'Collective guilt? This can't be true. That's a load of bullshit. What did you have to do with the crimes of the SS or the extermination of the Jews?'

'Nothing and at the same time everything. Not I as an individual, but I as a German. That's what I mean.'

'That's a bit far-fetched. That's the fucking Soviet propaganda you were fed in the camp.'

'Well, you may think it's weird. But when I got home, I felt in a way, that I had done my bit of penitence. Not for fighting in Russia, but for Germany.'

'Please, Max,' she interrupted, 'total bullshit.'

'No, Xenia, let me finish please.' She sat back in her chair again, leaning against the window, her arms folded across her chest.

'This repenting was real for me. Every day. Maybe it was

a way of rationalising away the cold and the pain we had to endure. The days when you saw your friends giving up on life, as they couldn't face things anymore. You know, you had to have a reason to continue living. For some people it was love. For others it was hatred. Hating someone is an amazingly strong motivation. For some few of us, it was this sense that we wanted to rebuild what had been destroyed.'

'How very heroic.' Xenia's lips dropped sarcastically.

'Of course it wasn't heroic. I knew that. But when I came back after those years my world fell apart as I had to realise that all those years we had been suffering, most people who had committed real crimes, all those big Nazis, continued running about just as if nothing had happened. During the Nuremberg trials only the biggest fish got executed whereas in my view, they should have convicted and hanged or at least jailed thousands. But thousands just washed their bloody hands and became democrats overnight. Like Hempe, everyone had only been a *Mitläufer*, just running along.' I paused and got up as I needed to walk up and down. I felt Xenia's eyes in my back. I looked at her, and her eyes were dark and serious. She took my hand and pulled me towards her. I sat down again. The train slowed down and we observed the trees of a forest passing by in silence.

'And still, even after your story, I have not understood what gives you the right to kill,' she said.

I wanted to say "the enormity of the crimes that our legal system is struggling with to punish adequately" but decided to remain silent. I had no right to avenge murder with murder. And yet I knew that killing Hempe and Odenbrecht was the right thing to do whereas killing the Soviet soldiers who were running towards us felt to me like a crime.

I had acquitted a woman who had killed her husband. After years of pain, beatings, rape she finally snapped and rammed a kitchen knife into his chest. To the prosecution it was cold-blooded murder. To me it was self-defence and ultimate justice where our justice system had failed to protect her. Self-defence could be held up in court – ultimate justice not. She walked free.

'Maybe the Allies should have kept Nuremberg open till today and kept sending all those Nazis to the fucking gallows all those post-war years.'

I had no clue whether Xenia meant it or not.

The door opened and a woman came into the carriage with a trolley laden with food and drinks. Xenia ordered a large coffee. She added some sugar and stirred it carefully, trying to balance the cup whilst the train was moving. She took a sip.

'This really is disgusting. You live so near to Italy and France but Germans are incapable of producing proper coffee.'

'Well, be fair. Coffee in an Italian train is equally disgusting.'

'Probably true,' she conceded. 'But coffee in a German café doesn't taste that much better.'

'How do you know? Have you ever been to a German café?'

'Yes, the day I arrived in Munich. Near the Marienplatz.'

'You should have gone to Café Kreutzkamp. Let's go there when we get back.' I looked at her as she was sipping the coffee and then said, 'I don't know about Müller. But you're right. That chapter isn't closed. But I'm not sure whether I will close it or whether I will leave it open. Maybe, if this chapter needs closing, he would have been run over by a car a long time ago. Or struck down with cancer in some cruel way.'

Xenia turned around abruptly. 'Jesus Christ. You know yourself people don't die of cancer because of some chapter that needs closing. That would be fucking unfair on Mischa. What's he done to deserve a brain tumour?'

'Nothing. Of course.'

'Otherwise Germany would be the country with the highest cancer rate,' she said.

I looked at her, as her eyes were scanning the horizon. What was she thinking about?

'Anyway, I'm not sure that you're destined to be Müller's executioner, but you can get him sent to jail. Siberia would be better.'

Mischa

When we arrived at the hospital Mischa was lying in bed, turning his head as we entered. He was bandaged up and looked spaced out, smiling vaguely.

'They didn't manage to kill me,' he muttered when we entered. 'Hello Max.'

He turned to Xenia, looking at her through half closed eyes. 'And you must be Xenia.' She nodded and took his hand and held it gently. He sat up. 'I'm sorry about receiving you here in bed. Why didn't you tell me, Max, she's coming with you?'

'I love surprising people,' Xenia said.

Mischa looked up, now fully awake.

'Wonderful. Such a pleasure to meet you in person. Max told me so much about you.'

I felt relief when I realised he could speak normally.

'I hope only good things.'

'Of course,' Mischa said, now with a charming smile.

Xenia looked at me and then turned to Mischa with a serious face.

'I'm sorry. I mean, my coming unannounced, visiting you over here. I hope you are feeling OK after the operation.'

'Nah. Just a small tumour.'

'I'll keep my fingers crossed for your speedy recovery.'

'Thanks,' Mischa said, lying back on the bed. He looked at Xenia. 'It's so nice of you to come and so awful to meet you here in hospital.' He paused and looked at her with a mischievous smile. 'You're aware, aren't you: You've changed Max from being an old misanthrope to a new-born person? I've never seen him strut around with that much energy, or interest in other things than just law.'

'Oh, come on,' Xenia replied. 'It's not because of me but because he is a free spirit now, a pensioner, no obligations, enough money and loads of time. What did you expect?'

'I expected him to become really grumpy, old and dying within the next five years. And now he's quite unbearable.'

'Oh thanks,' I said.

'That's what friends are for,' Mischa said. Xenia glanced at him and then at me, heading for the door.

'I'll leave you two alone for a bit,' she said closing the door behind her.

There was silence. Mischa's face was blank.

'Max. You're mad,' Mischa finally whispered. 'How can you do this? She's a child.'

'No, she's twenty-five.'

'Whatever, that's not the point. She's forty years younger than you, Max. I'm your friend. I have to tell you this: you are taking advantage of a kid. You are bloody insane, Max.'

I sat down, not sure what to answer.

'Mischa, I don't know what to do,' I admitted. 'I mean,

one of the reasons I left Moscow was to get my sanity back. I needed some distance. But distance hasn't helped a bit. I'm embarrassed to admit, Mischa, I love her. I'm not sure you can understand this, knowing me only as a grumpy fart. She loves me too.'

'You are exploiting her feelings. She is looking for a father or a grandfather, not for a partner in life.'

'So, tell, me, what should I do?'

'Be honest. Talk with her. Send her home.'

'She won't go, Mischa, you don't understand. She really loves me the way I am. At least she tells me so.'

'I don't know Max. But for heaven's sake, don't hurt her.'

'I won't.'

'But you will when you dump her, when you turn bloody closed-up again.'

'I won't dump her, Mischa. You don't realise. This is serious. I don't know. This feels like it felt with Julia, no, even more intense. As if our time is limited, running out in a way.'

'It is limited don't kid yourself. You'll be dying soon. And then? You will have ruined her life.'

'She knows my age.'

'But Max, don't you sense she's fragile underneath the happy surface?'

'No, she's not. Well. Yes of course I fear she may be. I don't know since she's not fragile in the way I encountered fragile people in court. She's a mix of extremely tough and then very sensitive. Look Mischa. I tried to not let it happen. But it happened. So...'

The door opened and Xenia re-entered.

'Holy shit, what's going on in here. You two look as if you're squabbling over your obituaries.'

'We are, darling, how do you know?' I said.

She went up to Mischa's bed and hugged him spontaneously.

'Have you had any breakfast? Are you allowed to eat anything?' she said.

'I'm actually a bit hungry, and still pretty groggy.'

'Sleeping pills?' Xenia said.

'No, Morphine,' Mischa said.

'Keep some for me when you leave this place. And look. We've got you a croissant,' I said.

'Not sure whether I'm allowed to eat this.'

'Oh, come on. Don't become obedient at your age.'

'Max, you're not allowed to eat anything after an operation. You're so irresponsible,' Xenia said.

'Oh, just a bit of croissant, it's nothing, Xenia. One bite,' Mischa said.

I got some jam from the kitchen and helped him eat it.

'You really were hungry, Mischa,' Xenia observed, when she saw him finish the whole croissant.

'Yeah, but not too keen on the disgusting hospital food.'

'Let's get him some pizza for lunch,' I suggested.

We stayed for half an hour until the nurse indicated to us that it would be better to leave Mischa to sleep for a while. We went out into the sunshine and decided to walk in the nearby park.

'When I was a kid, we had a swing like this in front of our house. I used to go there every day. I simply loved it. It's like flying.'

Xenia sat down on a see-saw, observing the kids.

We returned to the ward after lunch in the early afternoon. Helena had arrived and was sitting on the chair next to the bed. She got up when we entered and left the room to talk to us outside.

'I think he is so much better. It's great to see him so optimistic again,' she said.

'But he's still very weak,' Xenia said.

'That's because he hasn't eaten a thing. Or what he's eaten this morning he threw up again.' Helena was looking at us. I looked down.

'Let's go inside.'

Mischa opened his eyes again and looked at me as if slowly waking up.

'Do you know what I was thinking about when I went into theatre, Max?'

He continued without waiting for my reply, 'I was thinking about the day when you saved my arse, when we were all retreating under attack.'

'Sorry, Mischa, I don't recall. We were retreating all the time. And everyone saved everybody's ass.'

'No, Max. We were in – I've forgotten what that godforsaken place was called, but it was really early in the morning. We were all asleep in that village and shells were coming down everywhere as if the Russians were determined to erase the whole bloody place. The house where I was sleeping got a direct hit and the oven exploded, killing the farmer and his wife instantly and the house collapsed, trapping me under a beam. Then the whole place started burning and no-one came. And I heard the orders to retreat and shouted like mad, but the fire made so much noise that no-one heard me. And everyone was pulling back.'

'Yes, I now remember, Mischa.'

'And then there was this machine gun fire and Russian voices,' Mischa said. 'And no one came and the heat was getting closer and I was ready to pull my last hand-grenade and blow myself up.'

He paused and closed his eyes, shaking his head.

'And that's when they gave me the anaesthetic. And I wanted to shout, 'wait, wait' the dream has not finished yet, but the anaesthetist just stood above me and then I heard you screaming my name and when I woke up, a nurse was smiling at me, and for a moment I didn't know whether I was here or there back then.'

The door opened and Dr Rosenstein entered. He shook our hands and then turned to Mischa's bed to study the files before looking at him.

'And, so, how are things with you?'

'I think we'd better leave them alone for a bit,' Xenia said, taking my hand, pulling me towards the door.

'We are just in the waiting room down the corridor,' I said as we left them. But it was only a few minutes later that Dr Rosenstein put his head through the door.

'Well, looks all pretty good so far. I don't expect him to stay here for too long.'

'That's great news.' I said.

'But you should let him rest a bit,' he said as he was leaving the room.

'You should probably let me rest a bit too,' Xenia said, stretching out on the bench. I could not sleep as Rosenstein brought back the memories of young Wolfgang to my mind. Wolfgang Rosenstein.

Rosenstein and Mompertz

It was strange. Rosenstein, Mompertz and I were born in the same city, probably within a mile from each other and when we were young, we used to be pretty good friends, all three of us. Wolfgang was in a way a cute kid, blonde, skinny, with blue eyes and quite shy. It was funny that he looked so Aryan. Mompertz, in contrast, was the son of a protestant father, fat, probably because his father was a baker, black-haired, of medium height, with a huge nose in his face and far too short arms and legs. He never knew his mother.

The three of us often went to his bakery on our way home from school. His father was a huge but gentle, elderly man, whom we all loved as he used to stuff us with sweet left-overs from his bakery. His son was kind-hearted too. At least initially, until he fell under the spell of the Hitler Youth, with guys like Karl Heinz Hempe and others.

Wolfgang was super bright. In fact, he was by far the brightest in our class. He was good at everything, except for sports, where he really failed miserably. Mompertz, in contrast, was not the brightest kid to say the least.

I simply ignored Wolfgang's showing off when it happened as I liked him and didn't care. Maybe because he was a good loser – I regularly beat him playing chess, which did annoy him a lot. But otherwise he beat us all at everything. He came first, then came the rest of the class and then, at the bottom, came Stefan Mompertz.

I was wondering whether I would have remembered them so vividly had I not killed Hempe.

My mother had come back early from the library. Lisa and I were hoping she would bring some pork schnitzel. We both hated sausages. But again it was just a meal of beans, potatoes and sausages.

I grabbed a book, Schiller, but could not concentrate. My ribcage was hurting where Mompertz had punched me. Lying on the floor, I had carefully checked each individual rib. None was broken. At least Wolfgang had managed to run away, I thought. But they had beaten him up badly, blood everywhere. That's when Tillman and I had jumped in, right outside our school. Bloody cowards. Two against one, two big guys against one fragile Wolfgang. I had kicked Mompertz's knee, hoping to break it but he was too fat and stoic to move. Instead he let go of Wolfgang and started punching me. I had managed to withstand the punches and landed my fist straight on his nose and next I had punched with my two fingers at his eyes and seemed to have hit them. Mompertz had been dumbfounded and decided to withdraw.

Thank God, my mother had not noticed anything as my face was not swollen. I felt hatred for Mompertz. And I dreaded the next morning when I had to face him again at school.

'Will you help me plant some flowers in the yard,' Lisa said, popping her head through the door. I never said no when Lisa asked me something.

We went to the ground floor and headed for the back door. A big red swastika was painted on the wall of our house. Who could have done that? The paint still seemed fresh.

'What happened?' Lisa asked.

'Mompertz and his friend beat up Wolfgang again. But this time we got them.'

'You have to protect him. You guys are the only ones he has.'

'I know. But we can't be with him 24 hours a day, can we?'

Lisa spat at the swastika.

A month passed somewhat in truce. We walked Wolfgang to school and then again home. We did homework together and, defiantly, visited baker Mompertz.

'Have an extra one of this, kiddo,' baker Mompertz used to say to Wolfgang, handing him extra-large portions of raisin cake he knew Wolfgang loved.

But then in November, our caution slipped. I had to help my mother and Wolfgang had to sit a detention at school and was walking home alone. He was kicked in the face, the stomach and became unconscious. He was found only hours later by his parents who were searching for him, lying completely drenched in the gutter, half frozen. I visited Wolfgang the following day. He was in bed at home, his face swollen, hardly able to look out of his eyes.

'I'm OK,' he said. 'Just some stomach pain. It will pass.'

'I will beat Mompertz up,' I said in anger.

'No, please Max. Just let it be. It wasn't that bad.'

'You were unconscious. Why aren't you going to hospital?'

'Look, Dad is a doctor. He knows. And the hospital is full of Nazis.'

'Hmm,' was all I could say. I stayed with him the whole evening and left late to go home. I was furious, both about Stefan Mompertz and his mates and about myself and the rest of us, that we were in a way unable to stand up for Wolfgang, unable to protect him properly. I swore to myself never to let this happen again, but to protect him in the future, even if that meant getting beaten up again myself.

The next night I went to bed early, skipping dinner. I was bitter and angry and put the pillow over my head to stop the noise from the street from intruding. It got louder. Finally, I noticed the banging was from the door. Lisa was shouting and banging at my door which I had locked. I got up.

'Max. Look outside. Just look outside,' she shouted.

I opened the curtains. Our neighbour's bookshop opposite was ablaze. But there was no fire brigade. Hundreds of people were standing around.

'Stop, where do you think you are going,' my mother shouted.

'Help extinguishing the fire,' I said.

She grabbed my arm.

'You are not going anywhere,' she said firmly. 'Don't

you see what's happening? The Nazis are burning books. And the synagogue. And looting all the Jewish shops and businesses. You can't do anything against them.'

Again I went to the window and saw the masses, the swastikas, the uniforms. Then a thought struck me: Wolfgang.

'I've got to see Wolfgang,' I shouted, dashing out of the apartment. I ran down the street where the stench and smoke of fire was unbearable. Finally I reached the Rosenstein's house. Too late, I realised. The house was dark. The surgery was ransacked. I knocked at the door but no one replied. Slowly I walked back home. Home. Was that my home? I did not want this to be my home anymore.

At the corner I bumped into my music teacher. He looked at me with sad eyes.

'It's over, Max.'

Then I realised how badly I was shaking. He took me in his arms and I started crying uncontrollably.

We never saw Wolfgang again as his parents took a train the next morning and escaped to France and then, as I later found out, on to the UK. Wolfgang died on the way on the train as a result of his internal injuries.

The police did nothing. Everyone knew that Wolfgang got murdered by Mompertz and yet nothing happened. Everyone thought he should be jailed for murder. And also baker Mompertz heard about it. And then his son disappeared. Stefan did not turn up at school anymore. When I next went to the bakery, baker Mompertz was a broken man. Mechanically, he handed me the loaf of bread and returned the change. I stayed and continued looking at him. Only then did he glance up and recognise me. His eyes were glazed and apologetic.

'Where is Stefan?' I asked.

'He's no longer my son,' he said. 'I never ever want to see him again as I want nothing to do with murderers.' I looked at him, as he was glancing back at me with tears in his eyes.

'I understand,' I said.

Baker Mompertz started crying whilst his bakery was smelling sweet and of almonds, as usual.

Things were not the same anymore. Life continued, however, and I forgot all about Mompertz when I got drafted and left for the front. And after the war, I never saw Stefan Mompertz again, but baker Mompertz somehow survived the war and I remember that I passed his shop after the war. It had withstood the bombing and smelled as usual, sweet and of almonds. I did not enter but walked straight on. But Lisa saw old Mompertz walking in the park in the evenings, once he'd finished the day in his bakery and had closed the shop. She still used to buy bread, biscuits or cakes, which continued to be the best in town, even after the war. He never spoke to anyone, and never looked people in the eye.

I was suddenly wondering whether I had really finished Mompertz's story. The thought seemed weird as I had not thought about Mompertz since the end of the war. Even when Hempe crossed our ways, I never thought about Stefan. Maybe, I should not consider the chapter Mompertz closed, if I stuck to my own criteria. I realised I had considered the chapter closed a long time ago. Particularly as I had not really been involved in it directly myself, even though I had been a part of the story.

Lisa

We had pushed Hempe into the lake and then walked back to the hotel. I realised that this gave me immense satisfaction as I knew that I would have never been able to get him jailed. For what? Being a Mitlaeufer? Raping Julia during the war? Molesting Lisa? Being a member of the Stasi regime? Worse people had walked free.

The next morning, I took Lisa to the station as she was heading back home. I looked at her and realised she was ill. Decades of communist tyranny destroyed even the strongest person, and Lisa was not strong. She had very high blood pressure and the medication she'd been taken for years was showing side effects. I did not realise that this would be the last time I would see her. She had a stroke soon afterwards. Her friends told me that they found her sitting on a bench at a children's playground. They thought she was sleeping in the sunshine, a book in her lap. It was weird, in a way, as she was reading Kundera's *Unbearable Lightness of Being*. And she must have simply died there on the bench, without noticing it, without anybody noticing it.

'I know what Lisa meant to you,' Xenia said when I had told her the story.

'Lisa's funeral was immensely beautiful, with lots of children and her friends. It was not really like a funeral, more like a big children's party, with singing, laughing, dancing. Of course her friends were sad, but the kids livened up the atmosphere in a way she would have wanted it. She'd always said that she wanted a happy funeral, with no-one crying and children singing.'

'That's very brave, in a way,' Xenia said. 'I mean, I don't want people to be happy at my funeral. I want beautiful music to be played, Brahms, and then people should just cry.'

'Well, glad you're not dying yet, Xenia,' I said. 'That leaves me some time to choreograph.'

'Oh, you're bad, Max. I really mean it. I'll be sad when you die, if I'm still alive. And I'll get you a big orchestra for your funeral.'

Back in Munich

Back in Munich, I enjoyed just being in Xenia's company, her inquisitive mind, her interest in museums, modern art. I knew little about art. In fact, I had never before been to the Lenbachhaus. Once again, I realised, I was a complete philistine, but Xenia tried to open my eyes. She showed me the paintings of Lovis Corinth and the next day we went to the Walchensee where he used to paint, and I found a landscape as he had expressed it. It was as beautiful in reality as it was in his paintings.

And every day I bought the *Sueddeutsche Zeitung*, Germany's more liberal newspaper. Xenia didn't read the papers.

'You tell me if something interesting happens in the world. I honestly can't be bothered to read about politics. I read a bit when the Wall came down. That was big news. But now that it's over, I'm not sure whether there is anything worth reading about.'

'But you've got to know what's happening,' I insisted.

'What for?'

'To be informed. One has to know what's happening in the world.'

She looked at me. 'You are happening in my world. And we go and see museums. And I get to play the piano and hope to have more concerts. Tell me when Castro dies or the US turns communist.'

Every day Xenia would sit down and write into a book.

'It's my thought-book,' she said. 'I write down impressions, thoughts, dreams. Stuff I enjoy or when I'm angry.'

'Something about us?'

'Yes,' she laughed. 'Loads.' And then she added to my surprise: 'Feel free to read it if you can read my handwriting. I have no secrets with you. I'd be surprised if you'd be surprised.'

'I will. One day, but not tonight.' She put her book down and came over to where I was sitting and kissed me gently.

The next day Xenia went into town to meet with another Russian musician who was visiting town. As she walked out of the room, she gave me her thought-book.

'Have an espresso and read it,' she said.

As she closed the door, I opened the last page. She had written about the light in the morning, how it inspired her. I flicked back to the days when I had arrived in Moscow and had first met her.

the strangest thing in the world happened today. a stranger visited babka and said he's from Germany. i first liked him as i was struck by his eyes. he is handsome and looked like a shaolin monk, i was thinking, weird. babka told me he went to see her as they had had an encounter during the war; immediately my attitude changed and i felt hatred creeping up; i immediately thought he was her rapist. we went to a restaurant and i wanted to find out; i sat down; he opened the wine totally calm whilst i grabbed the steak knife lying next to my serviette; i had ordered steak deliberately in order to get a proper knife. i was ready to hear the truth and then act; alas the truth was totally different from what i had thought it would be;

i'm such an idiot, i almost murdered him; it turns out he was the one who actually killed babka's rapist.

i'm sitting in a restaurant and look at him and have to hug him. i feel an immense gratitude towards this killer. he had the guts to shoot an ss officer; amazing. there are only few people with guts i know and he is one of them. i look at him again and feel this weird sensation, this being drawn towards him as i listen to his words; i'm trying to understand what's happening to me, i can't think straight when he is looking into my eyes – i feel naked as if he is looking straight into my soul, and yet this nakedness does not disturb me; maybe this intensity of feelings comes from flipping from wanting to kill him to realising who he is. later we sit and talk at the lenin hills and i sense this connection, this closeness I cannot explain; but when i move towards him, he does not respond. in fact, he seems to be quite distant, which i don't understand; typical monk.

I fast forward a few pages.

days have passed; we are in the hotel together; he's lying on the bed and i can see his heart beating underneath his shirt. and though i have peeled layers of armour away, i can still sense the protective guards and think, why can't i just go and kiss him and make love with him; he seems still distant and speaks about our age difference; what the fuck do i care; he isn't 85. i'm sure he can still make love to me; why is he talking as if i'm some vulnerable inmate of a loony bin; its fucking annoying – he's just like babka; why can't they simply see i'm totally normal and that it is totally normal not to wish to hang out with little 25-year-old baby boys but with grown-up men; max actually means something to me; i can talk to him; he listens and understands me; i can relate to him because of what happened to mama; but also beyond that;

I LOVE HIM. i just bloody love him, why doesn't he see it; why doesn't he... or does he? is he simply too shy; i think i will have to take the initiative; when they are shy, even sixty-five year olds behave as if they were fifteen again.

the days, weeks, fly, i've been practicing like mad and seeing max almost every day, we talk together, eat together at scriabin, walk together and i feel i slowly succeed in peeling away the last layers of his protective armour; i am so attracted to him, love him, his intellect, his history, his hands, his soul shining from his eyes, which i am now allowed to enter; we've kissed and he kisses so well; was it the lipstick that i put on to seduce him? i feel his chest and we kiss again;

I close the book. Why was I such an idiot to suppress my feelings, to listen to my inner word of reason that was so definitely wrong. I don't know. Probably because I was afraid of what the world would say. I guess, some people will still say I'm taking advantage of her. Well, so be it. I don't care anymore. I do love Xenia. I need to read another line and open the book again, searching.

we finally made love; i simply could not wait any longer as i was lying in bed, hearing the shower, i undressed and joined him, felt his naked body, felt the shiver down my spine when it happened and he showed his love – physically and emotionally; i don't remember much, just that it was both dream and such intense reality;

I close the book. Xenia took the initiative. Unthinkable how things would have developed had she not. But, no, it would have happened anyway. It was bound to happen.

Ten days after my trip to Mainz, the *Sueddeutsche Zeitung* reported the 'suicide' of the former SS officer Odenbrecht. The paper found it worth publishing a long editorial about the fact that some people are still struggling years afterwards with the atrocities they had committed during the war, wondering what had been going on in Odenbrecht's mind during all those years he was playing the role of a sober boring conservative local politician in Mainz.

I read the article to Xenia.

'If only people knew that nothing had been going on in his pea-sized brain,' I said. 'No remorse. No bad conscience. Probably not one sleepless night.'

'I just hope his good example will create many followers.' Xenia grinned mischievously. 'I wonder whether Mompertz and Müller will read the article,' she added.

'Mompertz doesn't know Odenbrecht. Even if, he probably won't be able to draw any parallels. He was too thick to think straight when he was at school, let alone in parallels.'

In a way I felt relieved as, subconsciously, I had been afraid that the police might start investigating and that some neighbours might have seen me leaving the house. Whenever I saw a policeman walking towards me, I tensed up, thinking that he might be coming for me, recognising me from some photo a neighbour might have shot. Now I felt free again.

Mischa recovered and could go home a while after the operation. When we went to visit him again, he was still weak and needed to undergo chemotherapy treatment, which is ugly.

'You look like a monk, Mischka, you should wear an orange gown,' Xenia said, seeing his shaved head.

'I felt like converting to Buddhism as this bloody tumour grew despite my deep Christian beliefs.'

I sat down in an armchair whilst Xenia walked over to the sofa as Helena entered the room. We hugged.

'Tell me, Mischka,' Xenia said, stretching out on the sofa, turning her face towards the sun that was shining through the window. 'You fought in the war. You probably killed a few people. I assume that since the war you have been completely peaceful, law-abiding...'

'Boring, you mean?' he interrupted.

'No, not quite. Just normal. What I meant is, if you saw by chance one of those SS arseholes whom Max told me you encountered during the war, and you could shoot him without anyone ever finding out. What would you do? Would you kill him?'

He sat down in an armchair opposite Xenia and looked

at her for a long time, thinking.

'Christ, Xenia. You're difficult. I don't know what I'd do. I don't think I could shoot the guy just like that. It's not my job, he'll be judged by God in the end.' Mischa sighed.

'If God doesn't forget,' Helena said.

'Actually, if you think about it, maybe you shouldn't rely on God's memory or God's willingness to mete out justice,' Xenia said.

'God is always conspicuously absent during genocide,' Helena said. 'I would shoot him.'

'A totally new side of my wife,' said Mischa. 'But I know I couldn't.'

He left the room and came back a few minutes later with a wooden box.

'Well, now that I've thought this question through, I realise I don't need these anymore either.' He placed the box on the table in front of me and opened it. It contained two relatively new, beautiful pistols, wrapped in greasy foil. I took one pistol out of its foil and looked at it. It was a Beretta.

'They work,' Mischa said.

'And you think I'll have better use of them?'

'Max. I've known you for so many years. I don't think that there are many thoughts you can keep as a secret from me.' He paused.

'By the way, I loved the book, *Stiller*, you gave me. I read it in hospital. It's such an amazing story and Frisch is such a great author. And, by the way, you left the sticker of the bookshop on the back of the book.'

There were a few moments of silence whilst he just looked at me before adding, 'Oh, incidentally, I read an article about a guy called Odenbrecht. It said he committed suicide in Mainz.'

I felt blood shooting into my head. Xenia looked at me and had to laugh. Helena was putting a disc into the stereo, oblivious to what was happening.

'Anyway,' Mischa continued with a chuckle for having caught me out, 'I thought these pistols are better for you than for me. I don't know why I bought them in the first place,' he continued. 'Probably just because I loved the pure beauty of the mechanism.'

'You're weird,' Helena said over her shoulder, still fiddling with the stereo.

Hamburg

We left before dinner and decided to take the train back to Munich. At home a telegram awaited Xenia. An agent asked her whether she was free to play a concert in Hamburg and, she jumped into the air, a concert tour in Japan: Tokyo, Yokohama, Nagoya, Kyoto, Hiroshima. The pianist Yevgenin Orukhin, had tendonitis and he had recommended her as his replacement.

'Yevgenin,' she cried. 'I can't believe it. I had a masterclass with him in January. He is, what can I say, just fucking brilliant. Poor thing. Tendonitis sucks.'

She paused, looking at the telegram.

'I'm too amazed to speak, Max. I mean, this is the stuff little girls dream about when they're sitting in their lessons at the Conservatory, but those dreams always go "puff" and then they are gone. And you end up as a fucking teacher of kids who hate playing the piano. Tell me Max, is this real or is it a hoax?' She laughed and dashed for the phone, calling the agent.

It was real. Yevgenin's agent had been instructed to track her down.

Hamburg sounded great, but Japan was an absolutely amazing opportunity, particularly as she had to play Beethoven's fourth piano concerto whereas in Hamburg it was Schumann again.

'I was becoming a bit of a one trick pony,' she said. 'I had always thought: better to perform the same trick in different circuses than practicing many tricks at home.' She looked at me from the side.

'And now you have to study two new tricks?'

'Will you come to Japan with me? I mean, if you can't kill Mompertz?' she said.

'Stop it, Xenia. You make me look as if I am a professional killer, with nothing else happening in my life.'

'Well, isn't that the case? What else is happening in your life?'

'You.'

'Well, that makes you a professional killer with a muse.'

'I'll think about it,' I said. 'I've never been to Tokyo, but have to think about Hamburg, to be honest. Not that I know the place very well, but Tokyo sounds more interesting.'

'Well, you haven't been anywhere in your life, so everything must sound interesting.'

'Wow. You're biting, Darling. Do I deserve this?'

'You deserve a lot more,' she said and came over and kissed me.

Later we had dinner at Sergio's. Sergio came out of the kitchen and joined us at the table.

'So Dottore,' he said. 'When will you start teaching?'

Xenia looked at me. 'You haven't told me. Teach what?'

'I've also been asked, whether I'd be interested in teaching criminal law.'

Xenia laughed out loud. Sergio smiled and turned to greet entering customers.

'Holy fuck. That's so funny. The criminal, teaching criminal law.'

'Shht. Xenia. Please. It's not funny.'

'Oh, come on, it is. Really. Well, perhaps ironic is the better term.'

'By the way, Xenia,' I said, trying to change the topic. 'Which do you prefer: Boesendorfer, Steinway, Bechstein, or Yamaha.'

'Christ, not a fucking Yamaha. How about a Suzuki? No, really,' she said as she dived into her food. 'I really don't know. I love Steinway, but only the really long grands. Crystal clear sound. But then Boesendorfer has a much richer sound, particularly the lower notes. I played a Boesendorfer in Munich. But I also love Bechsteins. They have such an earthy sound. And you don't need a grand to get a good volume. At the Conservatory I play on a Steinway or a Bechstein.'

'Thanks, Xenia.' I said. 'That was very clear and your choice was very well argued.'

'Oh, bloody hell. I'm not a lawyer. If you knew a bit more about music, you'd have the same preferences and couldn't decide on one. Menuhin had a whole collection of Stradivari. He changed, if you'd really like to know, depending on his mood or the size of the concert hall or the piece he was playing. Look. When I play Rachmaninoff, I prefer a Bechstein. Schumann on a Boesendorfer. Beethoven on Steinway. But I can play anything on any Honda,' she laughed at me disarmingly and added: 'But why do you ask?'

'Just asking.'

The next morning we headed into town to do some window-shopping. We were walking pretty aimlessly until we stopped in front of the window of Piano Fischer, a beautiful building with huge windows. We entered. In front of us was a huge selection of pianos. Xenia sat down at the nearest one and started playing. Chopin, then Brahms. She got up and moved to the next one. Debussy. Next Bach, Kunst der Fuge and more Chopin. I decided to sit down and enjoy the cappuccino the elderly sales lady made for us. After half an hour I went out to call Mischa who sounded a bit better. When I returned, Xenia was still in front of the same piano, a pitch black Bechstein baby grand.

'This is a wonderful instrument. Just listen, Max. Let me play you some Bach to start off with.'

She played four counterpoints with closed eyes in full concentration, almost as if listening to how the sound she was playing was developing in the air.

'And now, listen to this contrast.' And she hammered away.

'What is it?'

'Rachmaninoff, of course!' she said without looking up. 'I love it. Just listen, the clarity and power of those lower notes.'

The shop assistant came over and stared at Xenia. 'She is amazing. Only Richter can play like her. He once came in and played Rachmaninoff right over here.'

I bought the Bechstein and left a set of my house keys with the shop assistant and asked them to deliver it straight away to my apartment. It felt incredibly nouveau riche.

We had lunch in a small Italian restaurant behind the Frauenkirche and sauntered afterwards down the Theatiner Strasse towards the Odeons Platz and on through the archway into the Hofgarten.

'I'm so tired and bloody lazy today. Dreadful. I feel I should be doing something,' Xenia said, sitting down on a chair in the café. She looked around and added: 'this is so beautiful, so geometrical, the hedges, the flowers, even the buildings surrounding the garden.'

'That's the back of the Herkulessaal,' I said, pointing at the building opposite us.

'She laughed. 'My sense of orientation is absolutely rotten.'

The waiter came and Xenia ordered Earl Grey tea for both of us.

Despite her restlessness, it was four in the afternoon when we got back. I looked into the letterbox and found my keys. Xenia opened the door and went into the living room.

'Max,' she cried, taking my arm.

'Happy Birthday,' I said.

'But it's not my birthday.'

'Who cares. You need to practice and I love your evening entertainment.'

She sat down and started playing Jazz. I was glad that my neighbour below was practically deaf and the one underneath her loved music and surely would not object. The piano had an amazing sound, even in the confines of the living room.

She played the whole of the next day, mainly Schumann, the concert she was going to play in Hamburg.

'I think I'll be OK,' she said, closing the lid of the piano. 'I've been practicing this for ages back in Moscow.'

'I guess you know it by heart?'

'Of course. Well, actually not by heart. My fingers know it. They know how to play it automatically, but my brain or my heart don't. It's sort of strange.'

'Finger memory?'

'Well, it's actually not a question of just knowing it by heart, but of making sure that you play it exactly the way you want to play it. That's the difficult bit. You know, everyone plays concerts differently, well, not everyone, you have some dorks who just play, technically perfect, but otherwise bog-standard. But then great musicians have their own interpretation, like Radu Lupu or Sviatoslav Richter. I mean, there are hundreds of others, but I think these two really stand out.' She paused, reflecting. 'Well, in a way, I don't want to be a bog-standard pianist,' she continued. 'I have my own ideas of how a piece needs to be played, how every note has to sound, how it has to fit in with the orchestra,' she said. 'I can hear it in my head, and it is different from the way others play it. I mean, it's not easy to get your fingers to play exactly the way you want them to play. So, yes, every muscle has to remember how every note has to be played.'

The next morning, Xenia took an early train for Hamburg.

Innsbruck

The moment her train had left the station, it struck me. What an idiot was I to let her go alone to such an important event, where she needed my support. I felt mean and heartless. Here was a woman whom I loved dearly, and I was falling back into my normal grumpy behavioural patterns. I should shoot myself rather than Mompertz. Walking towards the post office, I passed a travel agent, went in and booked myself on to next day's late afternoon Lufthansa flight to Hamburg. In the post office I started searching the telephone books. Mompertz Bakery. There were hundreds of yellow pages to go through. Nothing. Then it dawned on me that Mompertz might still be living in East Germany, so I searched every city over there. There were many Mompertzes but not that many bakeries. It was not as straight forward as searching in West Germany, as bakeries had not been run and owned by individuals, but by the state, or kolkhoz, or whatever those units were called. I called a number of non-bakers Mompertz in Leipzig, Dresden and Berlin randomly, with no success at all. Disillusioned I went home and to bed. The next day I was at it again in the post office. For some reason I was convinced that he had a bakery. I don't know why. It was a hunch. Maybe he had gone to sea and was on some ship. In order to increase my chances, I looked up non-baker

Mompertzes in the West too. There were many. I had become so obsessed that I completely missed the time and had not realised that it was way after three p.m. when I looked at my watch. I rushed out and took a taxi to the airport. We got stuck in traffic and when I arrived at the Lufthansa counter, the flight was closed. So much for my wish to surprise Xenia and listen to her concert. I felt rotten and went home.

At Sergio's I ordered linguine and a bottle of Chianti. Sergio came out of the kitchen when he saw me.

'Alone today? Or alone again?'

'Oh, bugger off, Sergio. This is not funny. No, Xenia is in Hamburg, giving a concert.'

'And you? Why aren't you there?'

'I missed the bloody flight.'

'That's awful. You should've taken more time and gone with her. Really. Were you that busy?'

'In a way,' I tried to justify myself, but Sergio interrupted straight away.

'Doing what? You've stopped working. So what can be more important in life than listening to a concert played by someone you're so evidently in love with?'

'What do you mean, "so evidently"?' I said annoyed.

'Well, that's pretty obvious to everyone looking at you, Dottore. You're a changed man when you're with her.'

'That's awful,' I mumbled.

'No. It's great. You're starting life, after all those years you were imprisoned.'

'What do you mean?'

'Well, look, Max. Let's face it. You had no life. I've known you now for ages. Every criminal you sent to jail had a better life than you because they had hope. You only had work. And now? Finally you've got a life and you've mucked it up again, Dottore.' He grinned broadly and poured himself a glass of wine from my bottle.

'I guess you're right,' I admitted hesitantly.

'But tell me, what's up today?'

'I've been trying to find an old classmate of mine. No luck in Leipzig, no luck in any town in Germany.'

'Do you know what became of him? I mean, what job?'

'No.'

'What did his father do?'

'He was a baker.'

'Let me think,' Sergio said, frowning. 'You'll find him, Max. You know, when you grow up in a bakery, you either love it or hate it. I mean the smell. It's bloody penetrating. It's so sweet, that after a while it's either a drug or sickening.' He paused.

'So?'

'So sons of bakers either become bakers again or do something different. I've had two baker-classmates and both became butchers. For the rest of their lives they couldn't eat any sweets.'

'Interesting philosophy, Sergio.'

He laughed. 'No, not a philosophy, dottore. It's true. Philosophy is about things that aren't true, but where people want to find truth. Bakers, butchers – that's all real and true.' He took his glass of wine and got up.

'Need to go. Lots of people ordering. Need to cook.' He turned around to go.

'OK. Ciao,' I said. 'We'll be back tomorrow. I'm sure Xenia will be joining again.'

I called Xenia at her hotel. The concert was great, she said. She'd be back the next day.

The next morning I was back at the yellow pages. Mompertz butcher. *Metzger* in German. I searched in every town in Germany. Nothing. At eleven I had a double espresso. What next? I tried the major towns in German-speaking Switzerland. Nothing. Finally, at 11.48 a.m. I had found him. Butcher Stefan Mompertz, in a suburb of Innsbruck. I knew it was him when I heard his voice on the phone. I hung up immediately and went home and found a message on my answering machine from Xenia. She was going to stay in Hamburg as the agent had asked whether she would be interested in giving a small recital too.

I called Sergio and asked him whether I could borrow his car for a day. At 3 p.m. I was in his Lancia on the motorway on my way to Innsbruck. It was a beautiful day, slightly misty. The motorway was empty, but I drove leisurely and after about an hour and a half the Wilde Kaiser mountains appeared out of the mist. I crossed into Austria and passed the road leading off to Alpbach. How often had I gone that route? I decided I'd go back there one day with Xenia. After another thirty minutes I reached Innsbruck. I parked the car and decided to walk through the old town towards the outskirts. I felt the weight of Mischa's Beretta in my pocket. I put on gloves and took the bullets out of my other pocket and loaded it. I had not tried to see whether it was still working. I was confident it did.

It was getting dark when I reached Mompertz Butchershop. The front door was locked and I walked around the house and entered from the back. As I had expected, the door was unlocked. I found someone sitting in the living room, watching television. It was him. I knocked, even though the door was open.

He looked around and saw me and seemed absent-minded, if not outright retarded, I thought. His face was remarkable. Exactly as I had last seen it, except that it had aged. The news on the TV showed flooding somewhere in Germany.

'We're closed,' he said, getting up.

We? So he was not living alone. He must have a wife. I was hoping that he had no children, but there was nothing indicating that children might be living in the house. I quickly looked around. There were no photos of any children either.

'I know, Mr Mompertz.'

He glanced at me, confused.

'So how can I help you? What do you want?'

'My name is Max Hardenberg. We went to school together in Leipzig.'

He observed me for a long time in disbelief. Gradually, things seemed to be coming back from some long-forgotten depths. 'Max Hardenberg,' he said. 'Max Hardenberg. Yes, you used to sit in the last row. Next to Wolfgang. Yes.

Next to Wolfgang Rosenstein.' He seemed perplexed.

'Max Hardenberg,' he repeated, coming up to me, grabbing my hand. 'My God. That's a very, very long time ago.' He shook his head, still looking at me.

'Come on in. Come on in. What a surprise. Do please do sit down.'

He turned around and shuffled to a cupboard. I felt the comforting steel of the pistol in my pocket. I was thinking whether I should take it out and just simply shoot him rather than spending the next hour talking to this imbecile but decided against it. He took out a bottle of schnapps and poured both of us a large glass. His hand was shaking slightly as he handed me one glass.

'It's been ages, Max. May I still call you Max?'

'Yes, of course, Stefan,' I said.

'You know, school...' he seemed to have lost the thread. 'School,' he continued after thinking for a while as if in slow motion. 'You know, I left school much before you. That is, I don't know when you left. But I left school in 1938.'

'But you were only 13,' I said.

'No. I was already 15. Remember? I had to repeat a year and already when I started, I was the oldest. I just wasn't as bright as you guys.'

'Hmm.' I took a large sip of the schnapps. It was burning in my mouth, and disgusting.

'I remember it as if it happened yesterday,' he continued. 'It was November 1938. I did not only leave school, but also home. My father kicked me out and I moved in with all the other thugs into an apartment somewhere in Dresden. But I didn't want to be associated with them anymore, so I left them a week later and just lived like a tramp, walking aimlessly through villages, getting jobs on farms, stealing, sleeping in barns, hiding.'

He poured himself another glass of schnapps and then he looked at me with his big ugly eyes.

'You know, I beat up Wolfgang, don't you?' He paused. 'And you know that I ransacked the Rosenstein surgery?'

'Yes, Stefan. I figured that it was you who killed Wolfgang Rosenstein. In fact we all knew.'

'Max. I don't know whether you will believe me. But I did not want to kill Wolfgang. Or maybe I did want to kill him, but once I heard that I had actually killed him I was all of a sudden struck. As if I got hit. Woken up. It was as if I awoke from a dreadful dream. But the only problem was that the dream had been real and I was the murderer.'

He stopped. I was amazed by his eloquence, which was out of sync with his dim-wittedness as I remembered it.

'I had blood on my hands,' he continued, having emptied his glass and refilled it. 'And nowhere to wash my hands. I went to talk to a priest, but he was a Nazi and wanted to forgive me straight away for having killed a Jew. I was so disgusted that I almost strangled him. I had to flee as the police came after me.' He hesitated and looked at me. I took another sip and emptied the glass. He offered me some more but I declined.

'Thank God the war started,' he continued. 'I volunteered and was sent straight into the middle of it, to Poland and then on and on. War was something I wanted as I hoped to be able to forget and, ultimately to be killed so that the world could forget and Wolfgang's death be avenged. But it didn't happen. I received medals for bravery. When we advanced, I was the first, not because I was brave, but because I was a coward, wanting to be shot.' He drank another glass.

'But I was not allowed to die. I saw my friends die, I got wounded, but nothing too serious. After a month I was back at the front. That's how I missed Stalingrad. And I could not commit suicide either. I felt that would have been real cowardice. So I went on and on, till the end of the war, when I got captured, right before the fall of Berlin. I spent years as a prisoner of war in a camp in Russia, but also survived that to return in 1950 to Leipzig. I went to our street, to our bakery and saw that the light was on. I remember looking through the window, seeing my father, but I was unable to enter. Something held me back, something like a curse, so I sat down on a stone opposite the bakery and just cried. I couldn't help it. I cried for hours, hoping my dad would come out and take me into his arms, but he didn't. Around midnight the light went off and everything was pitch dark and so I finally got up and left Leipzig and started walking once again, but this time south, till I reached Innsbruck. So here I stayed, became a butcher as I couldn't become a baker, as the smell of a bakery carried too many memories of my childhood.' He paused exhausted whilst I checked whether the silencer was correctly attached to the Beretta. It felt solid and comforting. Soon it would send Mompertz to follow Odenbrecht.

'I tried to find the Rosensteins, to apologise. But I couldn't find them anywhere. In 1968, thirty years after I had killed Wolfgang, I couldn't face things anymore and tried to commit suicide. Twice. But both times I was found by chance, once under a bridge, the other time here in my bathtub. Both times I survived and continued to be haunted by my memories of Wolfgang. Whenever I saw a young blonde boy, I thought it was him. But it never was. And I look at my hands and realise these are the hands that killed him. Every day I am reminded.'

He looked at me with his dark and slightly reddish eyes, which were immensely sad.

'You probably think I'm mad, don't you?'

I shook my head.

'But I think I'm mad. I dream of Rosenstein, their house, I see his face, his wide-open fearful eyes the moment before I hit him in the face, the pain when I kicked him in the stomach. Most nights. It never ends and I wake up sweating and only slowly realising that it's a dream, a never-ending nightmare. You can't imagine Max, how I dread going to bed, falling asleep. I am mad, Max, I know it.'

I looked at Stefan and felt sorry for him. This was not going the way I had planned things to go. Shooting him would have given him the relief he had been looking for, ever since that night in November 1938. Instead, he was haunted, day and night. Was the life he had been leading the revenge I had sworn Wolfgang Rosenstein I would seek on his behalf? It felt crueller than prison or the sudden death he had been looking for during the war.

He remained silent for a long time and then looked at me hesitantly. I was overcome by a feeling of pity. I needed to drink more and gulped down another glass of schnapps. It burnt in my stomach. We kept on talking the whole night, till he needed to go back to his shop at six in the morning. We bade farewell. We knew I would not come back.

I walked back into town, had breakfast at a coffee shop and checked into a hotel, where I slept until the early afternoon. My head was heavy when I awoke. Outside it was raining and my room was cold. I checked out, went to the car, took out my rucksack and put the pistol into it, taking the bullets out and the silencer off. I would not need it anymore.

I did not know anymore how to define justice.

Leica

I missed Xenia when I was sitting in my empty apartment. I went to the piano and opened it, trying to play a few notes. I loved the deep notes. I tried to press the keys to play a C minor. It worked after the third attempt.

The next morning I went into town to buy myself a camera and ten black and white films. The shop assistant tried to sell me a modern Canon but I chose a second-hand Leica M2 with a 50mm and another 90 mm lens for portraits and architecture. I wanted to take photos of faces and buildings, but only in black and white.

At three in the afternoon I went to pick up Xenia from the station. I put a film into my camera and attached the 90mm lens and started taking photos of people disembarking from the Hamburg train. Then Xenia appeared in the frame of my lens. She was wearing a grey scarf and walked leisurely, as if time did not matter. I took three photos as she was looking directly into the lens. She seemed confused but then, recognising me, came running towards me. We embraced.

'You're so cheeky, Max, taking photos like that.'

She looked at the camera.

'Beautiful. A Leica. I didn't know you take photos, Max.'

'Neither did I.'

'But, why?'

'Just like that. Because I felt like it,' I said. I was not sure either why I had suddenly bought this Leica. I had never taken any photographs during my holidays or during my trips abroad. But I loved old Leica's.

'You're weird,' she concluded.

'How was it?'

'Max, I'm starving. Let's go to Sergio's and I'll tell you all about it.'

'I've got the most amazing Rigatoni Arabiata today. You have to try it Max,' Sergio said, coming out of the kitchen to greet us. 'And it's great to see you back, Xenia. Max was miserable without you.'

We sat down, sipping Campari Orange.

'Max. It was great. I loved it. A fantastic orchestra. They really knew their stuff. Amazingly powerful. A great conductor, it all flowed, quite intuitively. Unbelievable. And the recital also went pretty well.'

'I'm sorry, I didn't come to listen to either,' I said. 'I have no excuse.'

'I felt you weren't there,' she said. 'But that's OK, Max. I sensed you had something to do.' She looked at my hands. This time, I did not feel guilty.

'I know what you're thinking,' I said. 'But don't worry. I didn't.'

'But did you find Stefan Mompertz?'

I nodded and filled our glasses with red wine from the Veltellina.

I told her the whole story. Xenia listened and only at the

end said, 'maybe you should have shot him, you know? Maybe he'd been waiting for you to relieve him and free him from his misery.'

'You're contradicting yourself,' I objected. 'On the one hand you criticise me for committing murder and then you seem to condemn me when I leave someone in peace.'

'But you didn't leave him in peace. You left him stuck in his shit with no way of ever freeing himself. That's cruel.'

I did not know what to answer. But then she looked at me and said, 'if you look at it from another angle, you've probably done what he subconsciously always wanted someone to do: just listen to him. You listened. And you came and took the weight of this secret off his shoulders. Freed him.'

I was not sure, but then, again, thought she had a point.

'Maybe I'm naïve,' she continued after reflecting for a moment. 'But you are committed to meting out justice where there has been injustice, Max. But part of this also means freeing those who have been in jail for the wrong reasons, or for too long in relation to their crime.'

We sat in silence for a while, whilst I had to think about her thoughts. She was right and we were thinking along the same lines. In the end, we got up, paid and left the restaurant.

At home Xenia sat down at the piano and played Beethoven's Moonlight sonata.

'Why are you practicing Beethoven now?'

'Because I can't play it,' she said, shrugging her shoulders. 'And in Tokyo they want me to play Beethoven's fourth piano concerto, not Schumann.'

'Tell me. How many concertos can you actually play?'

'You mean, like in a concert?'

'Yes.'

'Really well only Schumann. And Rachmaninoff's second and Beethoven's fourth, but only with a bit of practicing. I used to think I was able to play Rachmaninoff's third concerto, but I really can't stand the way I'm playing it now.'

'What's "a bit"?'

'Working with my prof in Moscow for about a month,' she said, looking up.

'That's quite a bit. And how about Sonatas and stuff?'

'Oh, loads. I've been playing those for a long time. Bach, Beethoven, Chopin, Debussy, you name it.'

'You haven't mentioned Mozart,' I said.

She looked at me, turning around on her piano stool.

'You're right. I don't think Mozart is one of my favourites. Except for his Requiem which is absolutely powerful.'

Beethoven

Xenia practiced for hours every day, passages from Beethoven's fourth piano concerto. I thought it sounded perfect, but she was dissatisfied, and the more she played and practiced, the more dissatisfied she became. Otherwise our day was routine. Sometimes she asked me for my opinion. I had no clue. I often took out my Leica and took photos of her practicing. I preferred twilight scenes, just early in the evening, when it was still light outside but she needed to switch on a lamp to read the music.

After about ten days Xenia closed the piano with a bang. She had been practicing the whole morning, the same passage. As far as I could hear, it sounded amazingly beautiful, with feeling, thought, introspection. But she hated it.

'Fuck. I just can't play this. It sounds fucking banal. Bland. As if played by just any Yamaha jockey. I don't know what to do.' She paused, looking at me. 'I know it sounds ok to you,' she continued. 'But it doesn't sound right to me. And I don't know what to do differently.'

'Let it rest, try again the day after tomorrow,' I suggested.

'No, Max. That's never worked for me. I'd start again where I stopped today. And I don't have that much time anymore before Tokyo.' She looked for a long time into the flames of the fireplace.

'Max,' she said. 'There's only one thing I can do. Go to Moscow and go through every passage with my prof.' She looked at me, almost pleadingly.

'Would you mind, if I left you here for a week or so?'

'May I not come along?' I felt slightly disappointed.

'No, I'd actually prefer to be alone. Is that OK with you?'

'And will you fly straight to Tokyo from Moscow?'

'Don't know. Probably. What's the point of flying back first?'

We spent the rest of the day hanging around the flat, she was packing her things into a big travel bag. We made love before the sun rose and I took her to the airport in the morning and watched her walk through the departures area, disappearing through the doors. I took a photo of her just as she turned around a last time and to wave good bye. Suddenly, it was as if a bout of loneliness was sweeping over me, it felt as if autumn had truly arrived.

I took the train back into town and went to the Lenbachhaus, looking at the Kandinsky paintings. A gallery is the place to be when you are lonely. I loved the colours and the effect they have on the viewer – at least on me. Why had I never experienced this when I was still working? Outside I took more photos of people in the street and of the buildings. Only now, after so many years living here, did I start noticing the beauty of Munich's architecture.

Black and White

Mischa called in the afternoon. As he was feeling worse again, he needed someone to talk to. I told him that I did not want to talk over the phone, packed my Leica and took the next train to Stuttgart. He was at home and greeted me, dressed in jeans and a jumper.

'At least you're up and running,' I said.

'Up, sure, but running? Probably never again,' he said.

'Come on, Mischa, don't be so bloody pessimistic.'

'No, it's true, Max. Things are actually ugly. Chemo, seemed to work, but it really attacked my system and then yesterday, I learned that they found new metastases.'

'Shit, Mischa. Sorry. That's awful,' I said. I looked at him. He seemed very tired and depressed.

'Come on, can you go for a walk?'

'A short one, sure. But not for too long,' he said.

We walked out into the park. The sun was hanging low and a slight mist seemed to be floating between the trees. The grass felt damp. Everything felt damp. I took out my Leica and took a few photos of the sun against the trees.

'I didn't know that you'd got into photography,' Mischa said. 'It's an M3, isn't it?'

'No, M2', I said and took three shots of him. I saw through the view finder the pronounced lines on his forehead, the thinness of his lips. Looking up, I realised that all of a sudden, his face seemed to have turned old. This was strange, as for me Mischa had for some reason never changed.

'Don't' he said, waving at the camera, when I tried to take another shot.

'Let's take one of both of us,' I suggested. I put the camera on a bench and set the timer, running back to stand next to Mischa. I put my arm around him and noticed how fragile he felt.

'It's black and white,' I observed, picking up the camera again.

'I had figured you wouldn't do colour photos, Max. For you all is black and white and various shades of grey. But not colours.' I looked at him. He looked amused. 'Max, you are so predictable, so two-dimensional.'

'That's an improvement. One dimension more than before my retirement.'

We continued walking and came to a café. We went inside and he ordered green tea.

'Is Mompertz dead?'

I realised that we had not spoken about this subject since I got back from Innsbruck. I told him the story. Mischa listened quietly and shook his head.

'I guess I'd rather have cancer now than continue living like Mompertz. But I'm glad you didn't shoot him.'

'I couldn't, Mischa'

'So, the only one left on your list is Müller, n'est ce pas?'

I nodded, taking a long sip from my glass of tea.

'You know, Mischa. I am not even sure whether I want to kill him. Ever since I met with Mompertz, I have the feeling that maybe one should let them live with their bad conscience.'

'Did Odenbrecht have a bad conscience?'

'Well,' I said, reflecting back. 'Probably not.'

'Exactly.'

'I think I should try to get Müller jailed. We need to get evidence, witnesses – you are a witness. Natasha is. We can get him locked up for good. I did not have that in the case of Odenbrecht.'

'I think you are right. Jail him. And if ever you come across Moll-Hellinger, lock him up too.'

'Alexander Moll-Hellinger. I had totally forgotten about him. Wonder where he is spending his days.'

'In Argentina,' Mischa said. I looked up surprised.

'How do you know?'

'I read something in the papers some years ago. It stood out as there aren't that many Moll-Hellingers in this world. It was in a scientific journal, and this Moll-Hellinger was running some lab near Buenos Aires. I don't know. Maybe it's him, maybe it isn't.' He finished his tea. 'I've got to go back. I'm really tired.'

We got up and walked back through the park towards his house. Back home he lay down to sleep. He looked peaceful. I took out my Leica and took a series of pictures of his face. Black and white was ideal, I felt.

Japan

The next morning I took the plane to Moscow, checked into the Gostinitsa Rossia where they greeted me like a long-lost friend, and then went straight on to the Conservatory. Xenia was not there so I left her a message and thought about calling Natasha, but in the end decided to go and sit in Xenia's favourite café.

I had not realised Xenia coming in but suddenly sensed a presence and looked up. She was sitting opposite me, sipping tea from a paper cup.

'Max,' she cried, when I noticed her. 'You were lost. You didn't even notice me.' She laughed and got up. We hugged for a long time.

'What a surprise to see you here. Oh, how wonderful, Max.'

'I missed you and felt like being with you, Xenia.'

'I missed you too, Max,' she said, putting her hands into mine. 'It feels like it's been ages. I don't know. It just feels weird to be without you. I'm so glad you came!'

'How are things? Are you making progress?'

'Yep. It's been great. It's now the way I want it to sound. Even you will hear the difference,' she said.

'Even I? That's showing a lot of trust in my musical aptitude.'

'Oh come on, Max. Don't be insulted!' she said, laughing. 'Look, your Jeep is parked in the side street outside. Let's go somewhere. I've just discovered this new restaurant 'Dom Blocka.' It's run by a poet who's absolutely mad about Alexander Blok.'

'And who is Alexander Blok?'

'Max, he was one of the greatest poets. Look, I'll get you one of his books. They are selling them in the restaurant.' We walked to the car and Xenia drove me through Moscow to the outskirts where we found the restaurant on the ground floor of an apartment complex.

'I've brought a bottle of wine. I always keep some in the car, as the wine in most restaurants I go to is pretty horrible.'

'Don't the waiters mind?'

'Nah. They know they shouldn't be serving their piss.'

'Gosh, Xenia. You've become such a snob!' I said, laughing.

'Only from living with you, Max.'

We entered the restaurant, which was simple but cosy, with candles standing on each table and photos of poets on the walls. An old piano was standing between two windows. Xenia was delighted as we arrived just in time to hear a cellist playing the last piece of his recital, Bach's suite number four. As an encore, he played the Sarabande of the fifth suite, a most abstract and beautiful movement. At the end, he sat down at a table and joined the diners.

I had missed being with Xenia, feeling her presence, hearing her laughter, sensing her touch. I wondered how I could have lived the last decades without her.

In the morning it was windy and cold and raining outside. We decided to have breakfast in bed, which was delicious and decadent. But at some point, Xenia became serious.

'I still need to practice for two days and work on some shorter pieces in case I have to give an encore,' she said, chewing her croissant. 'And then we're off.'

'Do you mind if I come along?'

'Max. Of course not. It would be wonderful. But I didn't – I mean, it's such a long way. Ten hours flight. Are you sure you want to do that?'

'Look, Xenia, I still haven't forgiven myself for letting you go to Hamburg alone.'

'Oh, come on, you had things to do.'

'Yes, things that had been waiting for over fifty years? No, Xenia, it was wrong of me not to come along to Hamburg. I really want to be with you in Japan, hear you play, walk the streets, visit temples, and after your concerts travel a bit.' She looked into my eyes and then drew me towards her. We lay for a long time, embraced.

'I don't think I deserve this, Max,' she whispered.

'No, you've got it wrong, darling. It's me who doesn't deserve this,' I said.

The next two days flew by. It was raining most of the time and the wind let us feel the cold. Xenia was practicing and I met up with Natasha to talk, but our talk ended in recriminations and tears. I felt like hugging her, but then I realised that I could not do this as I was the cause of her anger and despair.

The city felt strange as if I had been away for years. Having a camera makes you observe people more closely, their facial expressions. You guess their feelings, joy reflected in the eyes, sadness, bitterness, some older people looked haggard. Why had I not observed these details before? I took photos of all of them. I loved the metallic sound of the shutter.

Natasha accompanied us to the airport, where she hugged Xenia and only briefly shook my hand. When I saw her faint smile, I spontaneously hugged her and she pressed her head against my chest. No idea whether I was forgiven.

We took an Aeroflot plane straight to Tokyo. It was uncomfortable and cramped and we hardly managed to sleep at all. I had difficulty stretching when we landed at Narita airport.

The moment we had gathered our bags and left the luggage hall, a Japanese man approached Xenia.

'Madam,' he shouted, pointing at a big plastic card onto which her name was written.

'My name is Kamio-san, welcome to Japan,' he introduced himself, grabbing Xenia's bags and heading off through the doors. Outside, his dark blue Lincoln town car was parked. We got in and sank back into the soft blue leather seats. We must have fallen asleep as soon as we were on the motorway heading for Tokyo, as I don't remember anything, except for arriving at the Okura Hotel an hour later. It was warm and sunny. The receptionists welcomed us in their stunningly beautiful kimonos.

We had four days before the concert. Kamio-san proved to be the most knowledgeable guide one can find in Tokyo. The town has few street names. Addresses are difficult, if not impossible to find, unless you know your way around, know where some of the temples are hidden.

And still we were surprised that Kamio-san had never been inside the Yasukuni Shrine. We decided to take him along. It was fascinating to see Japanese war history with paintings of fighter planes attacking US vessels, with copies of real kamikaze submarines. And with paintings of soldiers, officers and Class A war criminals.

'It's like having paintings of Heidrich and Himmler in a gallery in Berlin,' Xenia whispered.

But Kamio-san explained the meaning of Yasukuni as a shrine for all the soldiers and that the shrine was not to worship war criminals but to think of the war and pray for peace. I looked at Xenia and saw some scorn in her eyes, but she kept her mouth shut and only said after a while, when we got back to the Okura, 'You know, in a way, it really is disgusting to have all those war criminals there together with the normal soldiers who gave their lives.'

'But...' I tried to interject.

'No. It's the same problem about the whole country. Japan has not dealt with its nasty history. No collective guilt.'

'Not quite true, though,' I tried to say.

'But look, Max. Even today they talk about "Korean Comfort Women" and some fucked-up politicians claim that these sex slaves did it voluntarily. It's vile. As a nation, they've not had any grieving for the bloody crimes they committed. No Hannah Arendt. But then, look at Tokyo today. It's more changed than Berlin or Munich. Completely modern, not a trace of history left.'

'And you mean to say that the buildings changed but the people didn't?'

'No, Max. Of course not. All I wanted to say is that in contrast to Germany or Russia, there has been no justice,' she paused to correct herself. 'Well there probably was, but what I mean, is that there hasn't been full justice in the sense that the whole nation has come to grips with its past. Which would have also meant chucking all those fucking war criminals out of war shrines.'

So here was the pianist, turned judge.

'You don't take me seriously, Max, do you?'

'No, wait. I'm not smiling about what you're saying. I'm just smiling about our reversal of roles. You're becoming the judge and you are far less lenient than I ever was. You haven't even asked the defendant for his views and explanation.'

'You're right. Maybe I shoot first and ask questions later. That's what we do in Russia,' she said and then added after a pause, 'I think I'll leave judging to you in the future.'

She looked piqued.

'In the end, who gives a fuck?' she said, looking into my eyes. 'These guys are dead and their problem is that they fucked up, got nuked, Tokyo changed, today's kids can't give a shit and life goes on.'

Moll

The telephone started ringing in the middle of our second night. I looked at the clock: 1.46am. I let it ring five times and then picked up the receiver.

'Max?'

I recognised Mischa's voice.

'What's up, Mischa. Are you OK?' I was anxious.

'Yes. Don't worry. I'm better. But the reason I'm calling is: I've found him.'

'Whom?'

'Müller.'

I hesitated for a moment. Xenia had by now woken up too and was listening in. Her face got serious.

'Where? How? I mean, Mischa, why are you looking for Müller?'

'Max, I wasn't out there looking for him. But you know, I had this colleague Tom Rehmscheid who moved to Ascona four years ago. He visited me yesterday.'

'And?' I said, getting slightly impatient.

'Well, you told me Müller probably lives in Ascona and when Tom told me that he met this weird guy, Walter Müller, whilst he was hiking, I knew this was it. Tom always goes walking in the mountains alone. So he regularly bumped into this guy and they started talking.'

'So?'

'Well, it turns out that Müller had moved to Ascona some years ago from Argentina, where he'd been living since the war.'

'Mischa, that doesn't mean he is The Müller I'm looking for.'

'No, but wait, Max,' Mischa continued. 'The story goes on. Tom told me that over the next three to four months they continued meeting and that Müller started reminiscing about the war and stuff. He was in Ukraine. He was with the Waffen SS. And then,' Mischa paused.

'What?' I now got seriously interested.

'Then Tom told me that they were talking about the standing of the SS today, and that Müller said that finally people realised that they had had a duty, a job to do. And that for that reason he couldn't understand people who still today committed suicide, like a certain Uwe Odenbrecht, whose friend he was during the war.'

'Oh fuck him,' Xenia shouted.

'Yes. That's him. One hundred per cent. Him.'

Mischa turned quiet. I looked at Xenia who had gotten out of bed and walked over to the mini bar. She opened the door and took out a small bottle of vodka. 'Two' I signalled to her. She poured both bottles into one glass and brought it over. I took a sip.

'I'm sipping vodka, Mischa. It's ice cold and yet burning.'

'So what? You know I don't enjoy drinks at the moment. Well, anyway. Look, I thought you'd wanted to know as soon as I found out.' Mischa said.

'Mischa. This is amazing. What shall we do, though?'

'Well, it's pretty obvious, isn't it?' Xenia said. 'When we're back from Japan, we'll go to Ascona with you and Helena and meet with Müller.'

Mischa was pensive. I could sense him thinking at the other end of the line.

'I'd actually cherish the idea of getting him jailed, Mischa,' I said. 'Remember Dürrenmatt's *Die Panne*? We can have dinner with him and then interrogate him, push him into a corner and at the end, after the last cognac, lock him up.'

Xenia's eyes were mischievous.

'Please tell Tom that you're coming to see him with Helena and two friends?'

'Sure.'

'Wait, wait, Mischa. Don't hang up. Far more important, how are you doing?'

'Better. A lot better. Thanks. More when you're back. Good night.'

He hung up.

'When I hear what Müller said about Odenbrecht, I understand what you mean by "open chapters". What a fucked-up mind.' She paused and looked into the distance. 'Let's Dürrenmatt him. I like that idea.'

When Xenia had gone to practice the next morning, I went to the Concierge and asked him to find the telephone number of Alexander Moll-Hellinger in Buenos Aires or in the suburbs. I thought if someone would be able to find him, it's a Japanese concierge.

The orchestra arrived later in the afternoon and almost immediately started rehearsing. I decided not to join them but to walk around Omote Sando, taking photos instead. Xenia came back only after dinner with the orchestra, happy about how things went. The next evening was going to be the first concert of the series. I tried to see whether she was nervous, but she exuded an almost zen-like calm. She joined me in bed and we kept the door to the balcony open feeling the fresh air and listening to the artificial waterfall in the Okura garden.

It was me who was slightly nervous when I stepped into the concert hall. I sat down and looked around. Almost everybody was beautifully dressed, the women wearing jewellery, understated elegance. Next to me sat an elderly couple in their seventies, both with distinguished features, the gentleman had long white hair. He bowed slightly forward when I took my seat. The musicians entered and started tuning their instruments. Through the noise I could hear the flute practicing a passage of the piano concerto. The moment the conductor arrived, he started, having bowed ever so briefly to the audience. Egmont. What power.

Xenia entered, dressed in a long black silk dress, wearing no jewellery. She walked up to the piano, as if unawares of her surroundings, kissed the conductor, bowed to the audience, looked at me for a nano-second and sat down, closing her eyes. And then she began playing with immense subtlety, as if in trance, hardly looking at the conductor, sensing his every movement. She played with incredible contrast, the most subtle pianissimos one could imagine and then, again, hammering with utmost force, almost with brutality. The second movement was beautifully melodious but in the third movement she was back with force and speed, playing with closed eyes, only glancing from time to time to the conductor. I had to ask myself: was this still Beethoven, or was this Rachmaninoff playing Beethoven? The audience loved it, loved her and showered her with flowers. She looked at them surprised, then laughed with the conductor, shook the hands of the orchestra. The audience continued its applause and Xenia sat down behind the piano again, waited a moment and started playing her favourite Mazurka in C sharp minor by Chopin. Again the audience and the orchestra got up to applaud. She got up, smiled, bowed, waved and was gone.

After the break, they played Beethoven's seventh symphony. We listened to it together from behind the stage. Xenia was sitting exhausted, leaning her head against me.

'Now I understand why you wanted to get back to Moscow. It definitely was worth it,' I said to her, pulling her towards me, gently kissing her head. 'And the Chopin was amazing. It made me cry.'

'I knew you'd understand at some stage, Max. This is how I wanted to play but couldn't get it right when I was in Munich.' She paused. 'I'm actually amazed how little time it took you to understand. There are many artists who don't understand. Who'll never understand, or for whom this is irrelevant, whereas for me it is defining.' She paused and then repeated: 'Yep. "Defining" is the word.'

They started playing the second movement. She took my hand.

'I know this is your favourite and that I'm supposed to play it at your funeral,' she whispered.

'If you're around,' I said.

'I will be. But take your time.'

The next day we were in Yokohama, then in Nagoya, Kyoto, Hiroshima. Each evening a similar success. Xenia played with precision, power and feeling and was feted by the audience and also by the orchestra.

Hiroshima was the last stop and we said goodbye to the musicians after the concert as the orchestra was heading back to Europe. We went into town that morning, visiting the place where the unthinkable had happened, the epicentre of destruction. We saw the photographs, the monument, read the stories of the survivors. Xenia hugged me for a long time, tears flowing freely from her eyes.

'Max. This is just unbelievable. You've read about it, you know what destruction there was, but yet, when you actually see the place, the photos of the suffering, it's just so incredible. You know, nuclear war today would mean the end of our cultures. Of Beethoven, Blok, Rothko. It's beyond comprehension. Total Death.'

When we got back to the Okura in Tokyo the concierge handed me a note on which he had meticulously written down Alexander Moll-Hellinger's home address, telephone number and other details. When I thanked him his face turned sad. 'I've checked the number, Dr

Hardenberg, but Mr Alexander Moll-Hellinger died a year ago. I'm sorry, I hope he was not a friend.' I went to our room and dialled the number.

'Moll-Hellinger,' a female voice of an uncertain age responded at the other end of the line.

'May I speak with Senor Alexander Moll-Hellinger, please,' I said.

'May I ask who's calling?' the female voice enquired.

'Friedrich Fabelnstein,' I lied. Xenia grimaced. 'I'm a friend of Alexander, from Germany,' I added. 'But we've somehow been out of touch the last few years.'

'I'm sorry, Mr Fabelnstein,' the female voice said. 'My father died a year ago.'

'I'm really sorry, Madam. Please accept my condolences,' I said.

'No, don't worry, Mr Fabelnstein. It was time for him to make peace and be called by the Lord. He'd been suffering terribly for the last five years.'

'The last time I spoke with him, he sounded OK. He certainly told me nothing about his illness,' I lied.

'Yes, he was very brave, fighting cancer. My dad. I think the first time he told his friends was when they amputated both of his legs. Even after that, he didn't give up smoking.' She paused. 'And then he got Alzheimer's,' she added after a while. 'In the end, he didn't recognise anyone. Not even me.'

I didn't know what to say to her. Her voice was steady and yet it conveyed the need to talk about her father. I was in no mood to talk about Moll-Hellinger's slow and painful death on this long-distance call from Tokyo.

'Did your father ever talk to you about the war?'

'No. He didn't. Not once.' She was silent but, as I didn't say anything myself either, she continued: 'When I was at university, I did some research into his past, though. And I discovered why he preferred to be silent.' She paused again, and I heard her lighting a match. I could almost smell the cigarette.

'Did you know his friend Walter Müller?'

'Yes, I knew him. Dad and he were very close friends.'

'I knew them during the war, Madame,' I said. 'It was at the Eastern Front that I first met both your father and Mr. Müller.'

'I know Dad was an officer in the Waffen SS. And I know what that meant. But I still loved him. He was my father, and to me he had always been a wonderful father and he had so many friends here in Argentina. I guess, after the war he was completely changed.'

Xenia was beckoning me to hang up.

'I understand,' I said, and added, 'Again, my condolences. I need to go. Thank you very much.' I was quiet, waiting to hear what she would say.

'Bye,' I heard the faint voice at the other end of the line. There was a click as I hung up. I looked at Xenia who had been following the conversation.

'He was my father and to me he had always been a wonderful father,' she imitated sarcastically. 'A wonderful father,' and how many truly wonderful mothers and fathers did he kill? Sent to gas chambers or killed at the edge of a village? Pushing the still warm bodies into a dump, piling up wonderful fathers over wonderful mothers, covering their dead children. Holy fuck I have to throw up.' Xenia sat up in bed and reached over to grab a bottle of mineral water. She opened it and took a long sip and looked into my eyes.

'I know I'm a cynic, Max. But I just don't understand how such people, who go around murdering one day can be such wonderful fathers and friends the next day. After the war he was completely changed. Changed? By whom? How can you change like that? To be honest, I cannot understand the fucking nitwit daughter either. How can she love a person once she'd found out what a monster he was? Why did she not talk to him about the war?'

'Maybe it isn't her role to judge him,' I said.

'But, Max, that's exactly it: she did judge him. And she acquitted him as his positive sides of being a good father compensated for the negative sides of having been a mass murderer of the Waffen SS. That's judging, isn't it?'

'Hmm.'

Xenia thought for a while and then added, 'In a way it's her attitude which can explain why countries manage to overcome the horrors of their times. The monsters become wonderful fathers and people only know them in their new roles and not as members of the Waffen SS, or the Gestapo, or all those other little creeps who were just there to spy on you, denounce you, show where the Jews were hidden, open the ramps of the cargo trains on their last journeys to Auschwitz.' She drank again and got out of bed, walking towards the window, pushing away the curtains.

'I guess that's normal,' she added after a while with a quiet voice. 'That's what happened everywhere: in Germany, Japan, in Russia after Stalin, in Cambodia, Latin America. And, yet, it's so fucking revolting.'

She came over to where I was still sitting on the bed and took my head into her hands.

'At least, you won't have to fly to Buenos Aires anymore. Maybe,' she added, 'we can go there one day and learn how to dance tango. But we won't have to kill anyone, which is a relief. That is unless you want to clean up the Argentine Catholic church.'

I was not sure whether she was serious or joking.

The next morning Kamio-san drove us to Narita. In the plane we fell asleep before lunch over the Sea of Japan and slept all the way across Siberia. When we woke up some seven hours later, we were still flying over forests, valleys and marshes, Siberia stretched endlessly underneath us.

'That's our justice system,' Xenia said, pointing at an endless forest. 'Ruthlessly desolate and desperate hopelessness.' She took my hand and pressed it. Somewhere down there, I had spent five years of my life.

We didn't stay long in Moscow, just visiting Natasha, who had been studying the newspapers to read about her granddaughter's concerts.

'I'm sure there was nothing in the Russian papers, Babka,' Xenia said.

'No, you're wrong, Dear. Even *Izvestia* wrote about you.'

'I'm honoured,' Xenia said, smiling sarcastically.

'Oh, you are cruel, Xenia. You can't imagine how much that means to me. Please don't take away this happiness,'

'I'm sorry, Babka,' Xenia said, walking over to her grandmother, taking her into her arms. 'We're soon off again, Babka. I'm really sorry to be leaving you alone all the time. But I'm going to be living in Munich with Max as soon as I've finished at the Conservatory.'

Her grandmother turned away and walked over to the sofa and sat down, her eyes focusing on the ground.

'I know, this is hard for you, Babka,' Xenia added. 'And I hate leaving you behind. But you have to realise too that I've grown up.'

'I guess I clung onto that straw that you would wake up and return and live with me again, which was idiotic.'

In the evening we went to Scriabin. Everyone congratulated her on her success in Japan. Two days later we were on our way to Germany. Changing planes in Frankfurt, we arrived in Munich in the evening, just in time to have dinner at Sergio's. At home I found a message on my answering machine from Mischa.

'Hi Max. I've talked to Tom again and have told him we'd be coming to spend a few days with him in Ascona. He suggested the last week of October, does that work for you? Let me know. Ciao.'

Ascona

I was happy to leave the cold wind and the rain, trying to postpone the onset of autumn as long as possible. We took the train from Munich, which meanders aimlessly through undulating hills until it reaches the middle of Switzerland, where the real mountains stand like a barrier to the South. When we arrived in Ascona, it was evening and we checked into the hotel, where the receptionist confirmed to us that Mischa and Helena would be coming the following morning. The windows of our room opened up into the garden with the lake in the background. It was clearly autumn, a southerly autumn, where the days can still be warm but the evenings are fresh and the nights are cold. I stood by the window for a while, taking in the calmness of the view. Xenia joined me from behind and put her arms around me, leaning her head against my shoulder.

'Promise not to kill Müller when you see him,' Xenia said half-joking.

'I haven't even brought my gun,' I told her, without looking at her.

'Hmm, that's careless,' Xenia said.

Mischa and Helena arrived the next day. He looked recovered. Tanned, bald, a big scar across his head. We hugged. I could feel though that he had become even thinner and more fragile, but his eyes were shining. He turned to Xenia, 'Well, congratulations. I heard about your concerts in Japan. That must have been an amazing experience.'

'I enjoyed it,' Xenia said smiling coyly.

Later, in the library of the hotel we found a gentleman, whom Mischa introduced as Tom Rehmscheid. He was about Mischa's height, athletically built, and almost permanently smiling. He seemed soaked in happiness. Tom was delighted that we agreed to join them on their outing the next day.

Müller

We had been walking for about an hour when Xenia stopped to admire the view. It was a beautiful day, sunny and cold. The lake was partially covered by a thin layer of mist and the leaves on the ground were still moist from the dew. The forest smelled intensely of autumn. We looked down and could see two motor boats crossing the lake, a rowing boat was making its way along the shore. Xenia was in a relaxed mood, smiling, holding my hand as we were walking up the slope, following the wide path through the forest. From time to time, when Mischa needed to stop for a while, Xenia turned around and hugged me. I felt the warmth of her body, the pulse of her heartbeat. Tom had already gone ahead to the restaurant as he needed the loo and did not want to disappear behind the bushes.

'It's impressive, Miss, isn't it?' Müller asked, turning to Xenia who observed him even whilst looking at the lake.

We had met up with him earlier in the morning and I was surprised that he had not recognised Mischa or me. I recognised him immediately. Tom had introduced us as his friends from Munich. Müller was wearing walking boots and a beige raincoat. His face was tanned and expressionless, even when we were introduced. I could not understand why Tom spent time with him, hiking in these beautiful mountains.

'Yes. It reminds me so much of the Caucasus,' Xenia said.

'And are you from the Caucasus, Miss?' Müller looked at her, examining her features.

'No, I'm actually from Moscow, but I've spent many weeks there, in Georgia, you know?'

He nodded, absentmindedly.

'Have you been to Russia, Mr Müller?'

'Eh, well, yes and no,' he hesitated, looking at Mischa as if for support. Mischa looked at the lake. 'I was there many years ago, during the war.'

'Why don't we sit down for a moment now that the sun is out,' Xenia said, pointing at three benches that were standing in a semi-circle in the middle of a small meadow where the forest was opening up. The wood was still moist from the morning dew.

'So you were in Russia during the war,' Xenia continued, looking absentmindedly over the lake. 'Where were you based?'

'I was all over the place, to be honest. But that's years ago, and I don't remember it that well.'

'My grandmother does. As if it had happened yesterday,' Xenia said, looking with a dreaming and innocent face at the lake underneath us.

'I remember most of it, I think,' I added. 'I mean, not every night in the trenches or every house we destroyed.' I paused to observe whether Müller or Mischa would say anything but they remained silent. Mischa took out three

Cohiba cigars and offered one to Müller and one to me. He lit his, looking at the smoke as it rose in the still air.

'No, it's all too long ago,' Müller said.

'Do you at least remember Odenbrecht? Or Moser?' Mischa said, turning to Müller.

Müller looked at him with surprise and suspicion. He took time lighting his cigar. He inhaled and blew out the smoke without coughing.

'Someone killed Odenbrecht. He would have never written such shit,' he said in a quiet voice, almost whispering.

'Interesting,' Mischa said sarcastically. 'What did he write? And besides, how do you know?'

'The police asked me whether I had any idea whether someone might have wanted to kill Odenbrecht. I told them that as a former Waffen SS officer, Mossad was maybe trying to hunt him down. Or Wiesenthal.'

'Bullshit, Mr Müller,' Mischa said. 'Wiesenthal doesn't kill and Odenbrecht was probably too unimportant for Mossad. But I'm glad that you admit you knew Odenbrecht. Now, how about Moser?'

Müller was looking around, probably trying to assess whether it would be possible to simply walk away.

'Please, just remain seated for a while.' Mischa looked at him calmly. Müller got up.

'Please sit down.' Müller sat down.

'So, Moser. Do you remember him? He died in the war, didn't he?' Mischa continued, puffing his cigar. I observed him from the side, he was composed, his hand holding the cigar was steady.

Müller's cigar had gone cold. Xenia offered him a light.

'I don't remember how he died,' Müller said, looking at each of us.

'I think my grandmother's memory is better than yours, sir,' Xenia said nonchalantly.

There followed an eerie silence. Müller looked at us. I was tense but tried to look relaxed, like Mischa. We were still puffing our cigars. Xenia was rolling a Gaulloise cigarette. I noticed how Helena was observing things. She had not said a word the whole morning.

Sweat appeared on Müller's forehead but his hands seemed steady.

'What did you want to say?' Müller turned to Xenia.

'Just that I am Moser's granddaughter. Moser raped my grandmother and then got shot. The person who shot him is sitting right next to you, Mr Müller. Let me introduce him to you: Max Hardenberg. Judge Max Hardenberg.'

I glanced at Xenia and was surprised to see her so calm and composed. She had lit her cigarette and was inhaling, watching the smoke dissolve in the air as she exhaled. But I continued feeling tense, as I observed Müller on the bench.

'And I was the one who dragged Max Hardenberg away,' Mischa said. 'Otherwise he would have killed you too, Mr Müller, you shot him and wounded him, but you didn't kill him. He was the one, who killed Moser whilst Moser was raping this lady's grandmother. He was the one who shot at you through the window.'

'So, this is it,' Xenia concluded.

Again, silence followed as Xenia got up and took Mischa's Dunhill lighter back from Müller. She glanced at him coldly. His face was ashen as he looked at her. She re-lit her cigarette, which had gone out, puffing out the smoke. I had no idea what Müller was thinking, or how he would get out of this situation. This was not going the right way, I realised. I looked at him and was surprised how calm he appeared, even though I noticed his left eye was twitching. Finally, Müller glanced at Xenia.

'Well, now that you've started the story, let me put things straight and tell you what really happened, as you've got it wrong.' He puffed on his cigar whilst we were waiting anxiously. Only Müller and I knew the real story and I feared Xenia's reaction if he told it.

'We were in Ukraine cleaning up scum. Untersturmfuehrer Moser and I were driving past that pigsty which probably was your grandmother's home,' he said, turning to Xenia. 'We had been shot at by some filthy partisans earlier that morning, somewhere else, and felt the need to take revenge. So we entered the house and killed two women who were in there. We just killed them. And then we discovered the girl who you say was your grandmother. She was hiding behind the bed. So we dragged her out. And I raped her. I remember that one well.' His eyes were cold and fixed on Xenia. 'I raped her whilst she was crying, the dirty bitch', he continued. 'I raped her with all the hatred I felt for all that Soviet partisan scum. I remember ejaculating into her. And when I had finished, Moser was going to rape her too. But,' and he turned to me, 'you Mr Hardenberg shot and killed Moser before he could even get his pants down properly.' Müller let out a hoarse laugh. 'I'm sorry, I didn't kill you Mr Hardenberg.'

Müller looked at his cigar and started puffing again. The smoke rose bluish grey. I looked at Xenia who was staring at Müller. Her green eyes had become ice cold as she was realising the implications.

'So, you're saying that not Moser but you are…?' Xenia's voice was almost a whisper.

'Looks like it,' Müller smirked, nodding his head. 'Yes, I am your grandfather,' he laughed and paused. 'I would have killed your grandmother too once we had finished with her,' he added with a malicious smirk, 'had it not been for Mr Hardenberg shooting us through the window.'

There was complete silence. Müller looked relieved and puffed his cigar. The truth was out. I glanced at Xenia, who had turned white. Helena was ashen. Müller got up.

'Well,' he said, looking at us. 'It was nice meeting you all.' He turned to walk away.

'Sit down,' Mischa said. Nothing happened.

'Just follow my fucking orders,' Mischa barked at him. I was stunned. I had never seen Mischa like that, not even during the war. Müller stopped and turned around. Reluctantly he sat down again.

Xenia who had been staring at Müller turned and looked at Mischa with wide open eyes.

'No, Mischa. No,' she shouted, getting up. 'Don't Mischa.'

I too turned around to look at Mischa. He was sitting, holding a pistol in his hand. His hand was surprisingly steady. Helena was ashen, staring at Mischa.

'Sit down Xenia. Leave this to me,' he said with a quiet voice. Xenia sat down, trembling.

'When you had raped Xenia's grandmother and Max had wounded you, I could have killed you and I should have killed you,' he said, looking at Müller. 'But I didn't. I just couldn't do it. Sometimes I regretted it. And later I had been hoping that my regrets were wrong, that you had changed and had realised that what you did during the war was wrong. But listening to you now, I realise that you are the same inhumane SS swine you were when you raped Xenia's grandmother.'

I watched Mischa in fascination. I had never seen him so cold and determined. And I thought he had given me his only guns. He got up and started pacing up and down. Helena and Xenia remained seated but Müller got up too.

'Sit down, don't even think of running away, Müller.' Müller sat down again and put his right hand into his coat pocket. I was amazed how composed he seemed, as if at peace with himself and with his imminent death.

'Had you been just a tiny bit reflective, just a bit repentant...'

'Repentant about what?' Müller hissed. 'Raping and killing that Soviet scum? Never.'

'I would have let you go,' Mischa continued. 'But you're not and today I'm not the coward I was forty-six years ago. So...'

'Mischa, please!' I heard Xenia pleading.

Mischa turned his head and looked at Xenia:

'Please Xenia, leave it to...'

Wham!

Mischa's face twitched in pain.

Wham! A second shot. Mischa collapsed. I looked at Müller. This was the reason he looked so defiant and confident. He was sitting, holding his pistol in both hands.

Wham! A third bullet ripped through Mischa's body.

'NO!' Xenia screamed, running up to Mischa, taking his head into her hands. Blood was flowing out of his mouth. 'No, No,' she repeated.

Müller got up to face me. 'That was Mischa and now over to you, Hardenberg. So it was you who tried to kill me, eh?'

Wham.

I felt the bullet piercing my shoulder. It hit the same spot Müller had hit when he shot at me in the war. I felt a sharp pain. Where was my gun, I thought? It was suddenly as if I was under remote control.

'Well, you didn't get me then. And now I've got you, Judge Hardenberg.'

I felt strength seeping out of my body, my muscles gave way, and pain suddenly shook my body. I collapsed.

'Maybe I won't kill you straight away, Hardenberg,' Müller said. 'Maybe I'll let you watch how I rape again. Last time the grandmother and now the grandchild? Your mistress Hardenberg?' he said with an acid smirk, coming a step closer. He looked with deep-seated hatred straight into my face.

'Let me show you how I'll rape her. Painfully. And you'll have to just lie there and watch and hear her scream in agony and you coward won't be able to protect her. And then I'll kill both of you scum. And you too,' he added, pointing his gun at Helena who had crouched down over Mischa.

I had fallen on my side and tried to move but couldn't move a limb.

'Damn you,' I tried to shout but only heard my broken voice as if from a distance.

'What are you trying to say, Hardenberg?' He looked at me again.

I coughed and, in a daze, felt relief that I was not spitting blood. But then, out of the corner of my eyes, I could see Xenia creeping towards Mischa's gun. She grabbed it and, lying on the ground, aimed at Müller. Müller was slowly walking backwards, still looking at me, aiming his gun at me when she pulled the trigger, hitting him in the back. The impact threw him to the ground, his pistol flying out of his hand. Xenia got up and rushed over to Müller, picking up his gun. I could see Müller's face surprised and distorted in pain.

'But, but...' Müller stammered as blood was coming out of his mouth. 'My dog. Who will take care of my dog?' He coughed.

'Just shut the fuck up you despicable creep,' Xenia hissed and pulled the trigger of Müller's gun. Wham. The bullet ripped through his mouth.

'A tooth for a tooth.'

Wham.

Wham.

She shot into both of his eyes.

'And an eye for an eye.'

Wham.

Wham.

The last thing I remember was that I thought I could hear Müller's skull cracking. Then there was a deeply satisfying silence and the world around me got dark. I felt relieved.

Hospital

I woke up in hospital and it seemed to be morning. Outside in the corridor I could hear people talking. I looked around and realised I was alone in a room. Above me were two drips, connected to my arm. I tried to sit up, but felt a stabbing acute pain in my chest, which was bandaged.

I pressed the button to call for a nurse. A dark-haired nurse appeared after a while, wearing a blue and white uniform.

'So you've woken up, Dr Hardenberg,' she said warmly. 'You slept for a long time.'

'The bullet. How long have I been here?'

'You only arrived yesterday,' she laughed. 'Don't worry, we've taken the bullet out.'

'How is Xenia? And Mischa?'

'Who?' she asked. 'Don't worry, Sir, I think your friends are alright. But there is a gentleman who'd like to talk to you. May he come in?'

'Of course,' I said, eager to speak to somebody.

It turned out that the gentleman, who was wearing a perfect suit, was from the Canton's Police. He asked me in great detail about what had happened and I told him in great detail, including the story of the wartime rape. I forgot to mention Odenbrecht, however.

He told me that Mischa was dead. Xenia was still being questioned. She was pleading self-defence, which he appreciated. But there was no need to empty both guns and completely blow Müller's brains to pieces. He smiled ironically.

'What you say makes sense. And I understand her reaction. Entre nous,' he said, moving his chair closer to my bed, 'I would probably have done the same, had I been in her situation. It's only that as a policeman you learn to control your emotions and just shoot enough to make sure a guy like Mr Müller can't escape.'

'At least Müller is dead,' I concluded.

'Well, yes. There wasn't much of a skull left when we got to him.'

'I'm glad to hear that,' I said, with genuine relief.

'Well, Sir, you are a judge, and judgements should be in line with the crime committed,' he said, and again I sensed a touch of irony. 'Goodbye. I hope you'll make a quick recovery.'

I closed my eyes. Everything seemed to be turning black. I did not want to believe that Mischa was dead. I saw his face in front of me. Mischa – killed when he finally had the guts to do what he should have done right there and then – forty-six years ago. 'Mischa' I tried to shout, but he did not answer. I started crying and could not stop and did not notice how the hours passed.

Later, when it was getting dark, Xenia came running into my room.

'Max, I'm so glad you're OK.' She had tears in her eyes. 'They just let me go. I thought I might never see you again, if they jail me!'

'You didn't murder Müller. You acted in self-defence and in defence of me,' I said.

I looked at her, she was smiling faintly, her green eyes looking sad. I felt her cheek and her tears against mine.

'Poor Mischa,' she sobbed. 'Fuck. Why?'

I noticed that the room got misty, a dark heavy mist, bringing on total blackness.

Epilogue

I don't know any more how the days passed, but they passed with an unstoppable speed. "Pass" is the right word, as I do not have the impression that I was actively participating in them. It was more like swimming in a gigantic river, like the Ganges, where you are drifting along as the monsoon continues pouring down, and you see planks, boats, people, dead animals, floating by whilst you yourself float along, passively as actively changing your direction by swimming is impossible.

I try to remember. I looked at Xenia, who smiled back at me, holding my hand, caressing my head, as she was sitting on my bed. But then I am not sure anymore what exactly happened. I got an infection in the hospital I was told later. For two days I was drifting in and out of consciousness and seemed to be floating farther and farther away. I felt this strong force pulling me under and it felt misty and comfortable. But when I awoke, I saw Xenia looking at me, smiling, and I felt safe enough to drift away, even deeper again. I felt how she kissed me gently as I was falling asleep but then an eternity later, I sensed an immense activity in the distance and all of a sudden, I was jolted as something like a bolt of lightning struck my heart. I felt immense pain and wanted only to die when a second bolt struck and all of a sudden, I realised I had to wake up to survive, otherwise Müller would have got me in the end. The pain faded and when I opened my eyes again, Xenia was sitting next to me. I was attached to even more drips and machines.

A week later, I was allowed to leave hospital.

The following week we went to Stuttgart to Mischa's funeral. I had to hold on to Xenia and Helena during the funeral. Both were wearing dark sunglasses, even though it started snowing. It was amazing. The snow was early, too early for this time of the year. At the end, we embraced Helena silently, as the snow continued falling in thicker and thicker flakes. Tears were running down our faces. When we left Mischa's grave and walked back to the exit of the cemetery, the snow on the ground was thick and white, covering all the graves, the flowers, the trees. It was like walking through a curtain that silently closed behind us.

Xenia missed her final exam but continued playing the piano, touring Europe. She made it a point to play only Rachmaninoff's concertos in C Minor and D Minor the next eight months. At the end, she always played Chopin's Mazurka. Addressing the audience she said, 'this encore is in memory of Mischa. Chopin, Mazurka in C sharp Minor, opus 63 number 3.'

Later we decided to move to Moscow where I had been offered a position as visiting professor for criminal law at MGU. We spent most of our evenings at Scriabin or Blok and loved walking the Lenin Hills when they were covered in snow. Natasha joined us from time to time. Müller's death seemed to have freed her of an invisible burden. At Scriabin I had the first exhibition of my photos – they sold surprisingly well.

Eight months after Mischa's funeral, our daughter was born. We decided to call her Mischa too. She was so small, with pale lips, and pale-green eyes.

I realised it was time to switch to colour photography.

Lightning Source UK Ltd.
Milton Keynes UK
UKHW041148080121
376638UK00001B/41